I AM READING

JOE LION'S BIG BOOTS

KARA MAY
Illustrated by
JONATHAN ALLEN

KINGFISHER

To Marian & Isobel
& Alasdair – J.A.

KINGFISHER

An imprint of Kingfisher Publications Plc
New Penderel House, 283-288 High Holborn
London WC1V 7HZ
www.kingfisherpub.com

This edition published by Kingfisher 2004
First published by Kingfisher 2000
2 4 6 8 10 9 7 5 3 1

Text copyright © Kara May 2000
Illustrations copyright © Jonathan Allen 2000

The moral right of the author and illustrator has been asserted.

A CIP catalogue record for this book
is available from the British Library

ISBN 0 7534 1034 6

Printed in India
1TR/0104/AJT/FR(FR)/115MA/F

Contents

Chapter One

Joe Lion was small.

He was the smallest in his class.

He couldn't even reach

to feed the goldfish.

"It's only me who

can't reach,"

said Joe.

He was the smallest in his family, too.

Big Brother Ben could reach
the biscuit jar, easy peasy.

Sister Susan could reach it
easy peasy, too.

But Joe? He couldn't reach it,
not even on tiptoe.

"I'm fed up with being small,"
he said to Mum and Dad.

"I was small once," said Dad.

"You'll grow bigger one day,"
Mum told him.

But Joe wanted to be bigger NOW.

"I'll WISH myself bigger," he said.

He shut his eyes and wished.

He was still wishing when

he went to bed.

But the next morning, he was

the same small Joe Lion.

"Wishing hasn't made me bigger," he said.

"I'll have to think of something else."

He went to the big comfy chair

where he did his thinking.

But what was this on the chair?

 It was Mum's new book,

How to Grow Sunflowers.

"Aha!" grinned Joe.

"That gives me an idea."

Big Brother Ben had a *How to* . . .

book – just the book Joe wanted.

He raced up to Ben's room.

On the bed he saw the book:

How to Build Yourself a Bigger Body.

Joe read through it in a flash.

To get bigger, he had to eat

lots of food like pasta.

Mmm! Yum!

"I have to work out, too," said Joe.

"I know where I can do that!"

Chapter Two

Joe ran all the way to Gus Gorilla's gym.

Gus was big. Very big!

"Working out seems to do the trick,"

thought Joe.

"I can't wait to start," he said to Gus.

"What do I have to do?"

"You stand on this and run!" said Gus.

Joe ran on the running machine.

Then it was onto the exercise bike.

After that, it was the rowing machine.

Puff! Puff! Puff!
Pant! Pant! Pant!

"Now, lift these weights, young Joe," said Gus. "Lift them good and high."

Joe's arms ached. His legs ached.

Even his little finger ached!

But he wanted to be bigger.

He picked up the weights.

He lifted them good and high . . .

until a weight fell –

CRASH!

"Yikes! It nearly hit my foot. That's the end of working out for me," said Joe. But he was still determined to get bigger.

"Now I'm not working out," said Joe, "I'll do lots of extra eating to make up for it." Wherever Joe went, whatever Joe was doing, it was: MUNCH! CRUNCH! GOBBLE!

At home:

MUNCH! CRUNCH! GOBBLE!

At school:

MUNCH! CRUNCH! GOBBLE!

On the bus:

MUNCH! CRUNCH! GOBBLE!

Even in the bath:

MUNCH! CRUNCH! GOBBLE!

"I must be bigger by now,"
said Joe at last. He went to
have a look in the mirror.
He didn't like what he saw.
"Oh no," he groaned. After
all that working out and
eating, he was bigger, yes!
Bigger-WIDER!

"But I want to be bigger-TALLER!"
said Joe.

Sister Susan had got bigger-taller
in just five minutes.

He asked her how she did it.

"I put on my high-heeled shoes,"
she said.

"Aha!" said Joe.

"That gives me an idea . . .!"

Chapter Three

Joe rushed into Ernie Elephant's shoe shop.

"I need some shoes to make me bigger-taller," he said.

"Boots are best for that," said Ernie.

Joe tried on lots of boots, but none of them made him as bigger-taller as he wanted.

"I can make you some," said Ernie.
"But it'll cost you, AND it's money
in advance."
Joe paid Ernie. "It's all the money
I've got, but it will be worth it,"
said Joe.
"I'll bring them round – delivery
is free," said Ernie.

Joe couldn't wait
for the new boots
to arrive.
But at last, here was
Ernie. Now for the
BIG MOMENT.

Joe took the lid off the box.
He took out his new boots and
put them on.
"This is more like it!" said Joe.
He went to show the others.
"Surprise, surprise!
I'm lots bigger-taller now."
They were surprised all right –
too surprised to speak!

Bigger-taller Joe could do lots of things
he couldn't do before.

He could reach the hall light. He turned
it on and off – just because he could!

He could reach the rope to swing from.

He could see over Gus Gorilla's fence.

His new boots made a great noise, too!

CLUMP! CLUMP! CLUMP!

"I'll call them my Clumping
Clumpers," said Joe.

"That's a good name for them,"
said Mum.

But the next morning, Mum said,
"You can't wear those things to
school!"

"I've *got* to wear them," said Joe.

In his Clumping Clumpers he
wouldn't be the smallest in the class.

"I feel like an ant that's turned into a giant," he said, as he set off down the path.

Today was going to be his best school day ever!

Chapter Four

Joe made his way to the bus stop.

"I like this bigger-taller me!"

he said.

He was closer to the

sky, and could feel

the sun better.

He saw the bus coming,

and ran to catch it – or tried to!

In his Clumping Clumpers he could

only: CLUMP! CLUMP! CLUMP!

The bus went without him.

Joe was late for school.

Mrs Croc wasn't pleased.

"I'm sorry, Mrs Croc," said Joe.

"It was my Clumping Clumpers."

"Can I feed the goldfish?" he asked.

But the goldfish was already fed.

At break, his mates were playing
football. Joe was good at scoring goals.

But not in his Clumping Clumpers.

Joe was glad to get home.

"Biscuit jar, here I come!"

He reached it, easy peasy.

Now to watch his favourite television

programme, *Super Lion in Space.*

But then Mum said, "Hang up your

coat, Joe. You can reach the hook

in your Clumping Clumpers."

And that was just the start of it.

Joe could reach lots of things he
couldn't reach when he was small
Joe Lion.
Like the kitchen sink:
"You can take a turn at washing up,"
said Big Brother Ben.

Like the toy shelf:

"You can put your toys up there

yourself," said Sister Susan.

Washing up! Tidying up!

"It's all I seem to do these days!"

said Joe.

But he couldn't do much else

in his Clumping Clumpers.

Later, Joe's mates were off to the park.

"Are you coming, Joe?" they asked.

Joe shook his head.

He couldn't join in the games.

"I can only clump!" he said.

"I'm off for a walk."

Joe clumped off down the street.

CLUMP! CLUMP! CLUMP!

But what was up with Geoff Giraffe?

"He looks like he's in trouble!"

said Joe.

Chapter Five

Joe soon discovered that Geoff

WAS in trouble.

"Daffy giraffe that I am,

I've locked myself out," he said.

"I came outside to pick some flowers,

and I left the bath running!"

Joe saw the problem at once.

Left to itself the bath would overflow

and Geoff's house would be flooded!

Joe spotted the bathroom window –
it was open!

"You can get in up there," he said.

Geoff got his head in.

"But my bottom half won't fit,"
said Geoff. "The window's too small."

"Leave this to me," said Joe.

He knew what he must do.
First, off with his Clumping
Clumpers.

Now, it was
Super Joe Lion
to the rescue!
Up the drainpipe.
In through the
window.

The water was rising fast –
and lots of soapy bubbles with it!
"I must act at once!" Joe reached
for the plug.

It was too far down.

He would have to go in!

He got up on the side of the bath and jumped.

SPLASH!

He couldn't see through the bubbles
and his breath was running out.
But he must get to the plug.
"Got it!" He pulled the plug and
out it came.
The water gurgled down.
GLUG! GLUG! GLUG!
Joe whooshed the bubbles
out the window.

Then he skimmed back down
the drainpipe.
He saw a crowd had gathered.
Mum and Dad were there, and
Brother Ben and Sister Susan
and Gus and Ernie and
Mrs Croc and all his mates.
They were waiting for news.

Quickly, Joe told them:

"Geoff's house is safe from flooding
by bath water and it's safe from
bubbles, too!"

They all gave a cheer.

"Hurrah for Super Joe Lion!"

Joe felt very proud.

He was Super Joe Lion – just

as he was. He didn't need his

Clumping Clumpers.

"My clumping days are over," said Joe. "Being me is best. I don't want to be bigger . . . Well, not yet!"

About the Author and Illustrator

Kara May was born in Australia, and as a child she acted on the radio. She says, "Even though I am grown-up now, I am still the smallest in my family, so I know just how Joe Lion feels." Kara used to work in the theatre and has written lots of plays for children, but now she writes books full-time.

Jonathan Allen played bass guitar in a band before he graduated from Art School. He says, "When I was young I wanted to be a famous rock star, like the one in the poster on Brother Ben's bedroom wall." Now Jonathan is well known for illustrating children's books . . . but he does still play his bass guitar!

Tips for Beginner Readers

1. Think about the cover and the title of the book. What do you think it will be about? While you are reading, think about what might happen next and why.

2. As you read, ask yourself if what you're reading makes sense. If it doesn't, try rereading or look at the pictures for clues.

3. If there is a word that you do not know, look carefully at the letters, sounds, and word parts that you do know. Blend the sounds to read the word. Is this a word you know? Does it make sense in the sentence?

4. Think about the characters, where the story takes place, and the problems the characters in the story faced. What are the important ideas in the beginning, middle and end of the story?

5. Ask yourself questions like:
Did you like the story?
Why or why not?
How did the author make it fun to read?
How well did you understand it?

Maybe you can understand the story better if you read it again!

Adventure on Skull Island

Tony Bradman

Illustrated by Rowan Barnes Murphy

PUFFIN BOOKS

PUFFIN BOOKS

Published by the Penguin Group
Penguin Books Ltd, 27 Wrights Lane, London W8 5TZ, England
Penguin Books USA Inc., 375 Hudson Street, New York, New York 10014, USA
Penguin Books Australia Ltd, Ringwood, Victoria, Australia
Penguin Books Canada Ltd, 10 Alcorn Avenue, Toronto, Ontario, Canada M4V 3B2
Penguin Books (NZ) Ltd, 182–190 Wairau Road, Auckland 10, New Zealand

Penguin Books Ltd, Registered Offices: Harmondsworth, Middlesex, England

First published by Piccadilly Press Ltd 1988
Published in Puffin Books 1990
9 10 8

Text copyright © Tony Bradman, 1988
Illustrations copyright © Rowan Barnes-Murphy, 1988, 1990
All rights reserved

Printed in England by Clays Ltd, St Ives plc

Chapter One

In which we meet the Bluebeards

My name is Jim, and I live with my family on The Good Ship Saucy Sally. There's my father, Cap'n Bluebeard; my mother, Mrs Bluebeard; and my big, bossy sister, who's called Molly.

And if you haven't guessed already, we're . . . *pirates!*

We do all the things that pirates do. We sing pirate songs and wear pirate clothes. We sail the seven seas, from the Sargasso to the Spanish Main. We land on desert islands. Life for a pirate family is one long adventure . . .

Except, that is, when I have to do my pirate chores. And they seem to take up an awful lot of a pirate boy's time.

For instance, every morning I have to tidy my cabin and make my hammock. And then I have to feed Trelawney the parrot, and Long John Rover, our dog.

Molly and I take turns with all the other jobs that have to be done. The decks have to be swabbed every day, the cannons polished, the rigging checked, the sails put out or furled, and the anchor dropped or weighed.

My favourite job is going up into the crow's nest to be on watch. But Molly likes doing that, too, so we're always arguing about it.

In fact, we argued about it this morning.

'Who be taking first watch today?' said Father at breakfast.

''Tis my turn!' I said, quickly.

'No,' shouted Molly. ''Tis mine!'

'No it isn't!' I said. 'Tell her, Cap'n!' (We always call Father 'Cap'n'.)

'Belay that bickering there, ye scallywags!' he roared. 'I'll decide for ye.

Molly, ye take first watch today, Jim tomorrow. And Jim lad, this forenoon ye can write up the ship's log!'

'But Cap'n,' I said, 'it's not fair!'

'I'll be the judge of what be fair, young Jim,' said the Cap'n. 'Now shake a leg! We do be heading somewhere very important today, and there's no time to waste!'

'Aye aye, sir!' I said. Molly just stuck her tongue out at me.

The first thing we have to put in the log every day is our position. I went to ask Mother what it was. She does all the steering and navigation, so I knew just where to find her – standing in the stern at The Saucy Sally's wheel.

'Request course and heading, First Mate!' I said (we always call Mother 'First Mate').

'Ah, Jim lad,' she said, peering at the

compass. 'We're just north of the Roaring Forties, and on a southerly course. Why don't ye cast your lights over the big chart in my cabin below? That'll give ye the proper heading.'

'Aye aye, First Mate!' I said, and went down the companionway.

There was a pile of papers on the table in Mother's cabin. I couldn't find the big chart, but I did find something else that was very, very interesting – a map of an island, with lots of writing on it.

It was called Skull Island, and there were other names, too. There was Cutlass Creek, Buccaneer Bay, and Pirate Palm Beach. There was also a line drawn from a place called Cut-Throat Cove to a spot near a mountain, with a big, red cross on it. And there was a rhyme in a corner.

On an isle like a skull in the ocean blue,
There's a real surprise in store for you.
Find Cap'n Smiley's treasure chest,
Then find the X and you'll find the rest!

It was a treasure map! So that was the
important place we were heading for . . .

I love looking at treasure maps. I love
copying them out even more. The log
could wait while I had some fun,
I thought, and soon I'd done a perfect
copy. But I hadn't realised how long it
had taken me.

'Ah, Jim lad!' It was the Cap'n,
standing in the cabin doorway. 'That log

do be taking a long time. Stir yourself, there be some swabbing to be done amidships.'

'Er . . . nearly finished, Cap'n . . . ' I stuttered, hiding my map. The Cap'n looked at me very suspiciously.

'Jim lad,' he said, 'ye haven't been a lazy lubber, have ye? Show me that there log . . . '

Just at that moment, we both heard a voice from aloft.

'Ship ahoy! Ship ahoy!'

It was Molly calling from the crow's nest. The Cap'n dashed up the companionway. I folded my copy of the map, put it in my pocket, and followed him. Saved by my big sister, although she didn't know it!

On deck, the Cap'n was looking at a dot on the horizon.

'Can ye see a flag, Molly?' he called out.

'Aye, Cap'n,' she replied, peering through her spyglass. 'And it sports crossed cutlasses!'

'Shiver me timbers,' said the Cap'n. 'I thought it were he by the cut of his jib.'

'But who is it, Cap'n?' I said.

'Ah, me hearties, 'tis the cruel and villainous Cap'n Swagg,' he said. 'And he's heading straight for us!'

Chapter Two

In which Cap'n Swagg makes an offer

I'd heard all about the cruel and villainous Cap'n Swagg, of course. What pirate hasn't?

Swagg and his scurvy crew are the curse of the seven seas. He's the most vicious and treacherous buccaneer there's ever been.

So I wasn't surprised when the Cap'n and the First Mate started running about and shouting.

'All hands make ready,' they yelled.

'Stand by to repel boarders! Molly, fetch the powder and shot! Put out more sail! Come about! Jim, batten down the hatches! Avast there, maties!'

The dot on the horizon got bigger, and bigger, and bigger. Soon we could see Cap'n Swagg's ship, The Sea Slug, very clearly. There was the flag with the crossed cutlasses . . . and there were lots of cannon, pointing at us.

It wasn't long before we could even see the cruel and villainous Cap'n Swagg himself, standing on the poop deck. He was tall and thin, and he had a big scar on one cheek. Stuck in his belt was a huge cutlass and a pair of pistols. Next to him stood a small, fat figure with a wooden leg.

'Who's that, Cap'n?' I asked.

'Ah, Jim,' he said, 'that's the evil Bosun Billy, Cap'n Swagg's left hand man.'

'Don't you mean *right* hand man, Cap'n?' I said.

'If you use your lights, Jim lad,' said the Cap'n, 'you'll see that Swagg's got no right hand. He lost that in a sea fight with us before ye were born.'

It was true. Instead of a right hand, Cap'n Swagg had a big, sharp-pointed hook. And as I watched, he raised it in the air and waved it at us.

'Stand by,' said the First Mate. 'They do be coming about . . . watch out for a broadside!'

We all ducked down as The Sea Slug swung round. But nothing happened . . . except that they brought down their crossed cutlasses, and ran up something that gave us a real surprise – a white flag!

'Ahoy there ye Bluebeards!' It was Swagg himself, calling out across the sea between our two ships.

'Ahoy there yourself!' called back the Cap'n. 'What be the meaning of your white flag, Swagg? Have ye surrendered to us already?'

'*Me* surrender?' said Swagg, with an evil laugh. 'I'll never surrender to a lubber like ye, Bluebeard!'

'Well, stand by for a broadside, then!' roared the Cap'n.

'Belay that broadside,' shouted Swagg. 'I mean to have a talk with ye!'

'A talk?' said the Cap'n. 'And what has the likes of ye to say to us?'

'Pipe me aboard and I'll tell 'ee,' said Swagg.

Molly, as usual, was all for blowing them out of the water there and then.

'You don't trust him, do you Cap'n?' she said.

'That I don't, Molly me lass,' said the Cap'n. 'But the lily-livered sea serpent's up to something, and I mean to find out what. So pipe him aboard . . . and let's be on our guard, me hearties!'

So Cap'n Swagg and Bosun Billy came aboard our ship.

'Well, well,' said Swagg with a villainous leer. 'So this be The Saucy Sally . . . and a right, tight, tidy little craft she be, too.'

18

'Cut the chat, Swagg,' said the First Mate. 'What have ye got to say?'

'Not so hasty, not so hasty . . . ' said Swagg. 'We've come to be friendly, strike me dead if we ain't. That's so, ain't it, Billy?'

''Tis true, Cap'n Swagg,' said Bosun Billy. He was smiling and nodding, but I could see that his eyes were roaming all over the ship. He seemed to be looking for something.

'Ha!' roared the Cap'n. 'There's no friendship to be had with a hungry shark like ye, ye evil-hearted traitor!'

'I do know we've been firm enemies in the past,' said Swagg, 'but what say we work together? We could be the scourge of the seas . . . '

'Work together, ye say,' said the Cap'n, rubbing his chin. He turned to the rest of us. 'Well? What say ye,

Bluebeards? Let's vote on it. All in
favour of making Swagg a messmate,
say Aye!'

None of us said a word. The Cap'n
smiled.

'All in favour of throwing Swagg and
Bosun Billy here over the side, say Aye!'

'Aye!' we all shouted.

'Fools!' shouted Swagg as we
advanced on him. 'Fools and
numbskulls! But mark my words, ye'll
be sorry!' They scrambled over the
gunwale and into their boat, and soon

they were rowing back to The Sea Slug as fast as they could.

'Right!' said the Cap'n. 'Run out more sail, Jim, and let's get back on course!'

We sailed off, and soon The Sea Slug was just a little black dot on the horizon again. But it didn't disappear entirely.

'It do look like we're being followed,' said the First Mate.

'I do think ye are right,' said the Cap'n. 'We'll lose him after dark though, I'll wager.'

But as it turned out, it was something else we lost after dark that night . . .

Chapter Three

In which there is treachery in the night!

The Sea Slug was nowhere to be seen
when we dropped anchor. So we were
all quite cheerful when we sat down to
our supper. The Cap'n does all the
cooking, and he gave us our favourite,
salt pork, with plenty of mango juice to
wash it down.

After supper it was time to settle
down for the night. Molly and
I brushed our teeth, and the First Mate
read us a story as we lay in our

hammocks. It was called *The Lubbers*, and it was about a family who lived on land. They lived in an ordinary house, and the children went to an ordinary school. They slept in beds, not hammocks, and they didn't have to swab any decks or polish any cannon. It sounded very, very exciting.

Soon the story was over, and the First Mate said we should go to sleep. It wasn't long before I could hear Molly snoring, but I didn't feel all that sleepy. I got out my copy of the treasure map and looked at it for a while. Then I too must have drifted off.

But suddenly I was awake. I could hear something up on deck . . . a strange sound, a step-tap, step-tap, step-tap. I got out of my hammock and went to the cabin door to listen. Step-tap, step-tap, step-tap . . .

I opened the door, and was just about to go up the companionway, when the sound of a voice made me freeze in my tracks.

'Where do you think you're going?' hissed the voice. 'Get back into your hammock!'

It was Molly.

'Can't you hear that noise?' I said. 'There's somebody up on deck!'

'We must tell the Cap'n and the First Mate,' she whispered. 'They'll know what to do!'

'But how can we?' I said. 'Their cabin's in the stern, and we're here in the fo'c'sle. We have to go up on deck to get to them!'

Molly got out of her hammock, and we stood listening for a while. The noise was still there, step-tap, step-tap, step-tap . . . it seemed to be right above us, and then it faded. It was going away, down towards the other end of the ship.

'Now's our chance,' said Molly.

We crept up the companionway and peered through the hatch. There was no moon, and it was very dark.

'I can't see a thing,' whispered Molly. Neither could I, at first . . . and then

I saw a shadow slip towards the stern. And there was the sound again, step-tap, step-tap . . . We heard a door open and close.

'Come on,' said Molly. We moved quickly aft, and went below towards Mother and Father's cabin. When we got there we saw their door was open.

Molly looked at me and held her finger over her lips. Then we both peeped round the door.

There were the Cap'n and the First Mate in their hammock, fast asleep and snoring. And there at the table, searching quickly and quietly through all the maps and charts, was . . .

Bosun Billy!

So it had been him with his peg leg step-tapping on The Saucy Sally's deck!

'Cap'n! First Mate!' shouted Molly. 'Intruder aboard!'

Bosun Billy looked up in a panic, and stuffed something into his jerkin.

'Shiver me timbers!' roared the Cap'n as he woke up. 'What foul treachery is this?'

'Ye'll never take me alive, ye Bluebeards!' said Bosun Billy with an evil sneer – and then everything happened at once.

He pulled out a pistol, which went off with a bang, filling the cabin with smoke. The Cap'n and the First Mate fell out of their hammock, and Trelawney the parrot started squawking, 'Pieces of eight! Pieces of eight!'

Long John Rover bit Bosun Billy in the leg, but it was his wooden one. Bosun Billy tried to shake him loose, but Long John Rover held on so hard that the wooden leg came off instead. Bosun

Billy cursed, then with a hop and a skip, he dived through the cabin window into the sea. There was a great splash.

Molly and I looked out, but we could see nothing in the dark.

We helped the Cap'n and the First Mate to their feet, then Molly lit a lamp. The First Mate went over to the table.

'It's gone, Cap'n Bluebeard!' she said.

'What's gone, Cap'n?' said Molly. 'What did Bosun Billy want?' I had a pretty good idea already, so I wasn't surprised by what the Cap'n said.

'It's a treasure map, Molly me lass,' he said. 'That villain Swagg must have heard we had one, blast his evil heart. I did know he was up to something. That's why he came aboard . . . he wanted to see our layout, find the quickest way for Bosun Billy to get on board and down into the chart room!'

'And now he's got the map!' said Molly. 'What shall we do?'

'Er, Cap'n, I think . . . ' I began to say.

But the Cap'n wouldn't listen.

'Not now, Jim lad,' he said. 'All hands on deck! The sun do be rising already, so let's get under way and after those scurvy sea dogs!'

'But Cap'n . . . ' I said.

'Not *now*, Jim lad,' said the First Mate. 'Ye did hear what the Cap'n said.'

I was just about to say something else, when The Saucy Sally lurched, and there was a crunching sound. We all rushed on deck, where we discovered we had run aground on a reef. We looked astern, and there was The Sea Slug, sailing away into the distance. We could just see Cap'n Swagg waving his hook at us, and hear his cackle.

'They must have cut our anchor cable,' said the First Mate. 'Now we'll never catch 'em!'

Chapter Four

In which the Bluebeards face a storm

It was true, the anchor cable *had* been cut. We did have a spare one, but that wasn't important. What really mattered was the hole the reef had made in the bow, just below our waterline.

'We're shipping a lot of water, Cap'n,' said Molly after she'd been for'ard to check the damage. 'But it's not a big hole.'

'Whether it be big or little,' said the First Mate, 'it still do need plugging!'

'We need some spare timber,' said the Cap'n.

'What about this?' I said, holding up Bosun Billy's peg leg, the one he'd left behind in his hurry to escape.

'Well blow me down, Jim lad,' said the Cap'n, 'if that don't be a good idea! Molly, you see about getting that hole plugged with Billy's leg, and then we'll see about getting us off this 'ere reef!'

With a lot of sawing, and hammering, and slapping on of tar, Molly made the hull watertight again. And we didn't have to worry too much about the reef, either. For the tide soon changed, and

The Saucy Sally floated free of her own accord.

'Shall we put out more sail, Cap'n?' said Molly. 'Are we going to chase Cap'n Swagg?'

'Can't see as there's much point now,' said the First Mate. 'He do have a good head start on us, and we don't have the map any more. We wouldn't know where to start looking even if we beat him to the island.'

'But we *do* have the map!' I said, pulling it out of my pocket. Then I explained how I'd made a copy and hidden it.

'I should punish 'ee for not writing up the log,' said the Cap'n, wagging his finger at me. 'And ye'll still have to do it . . . But instead I'll kiss 'ee for saving our bacon!'

'Ye do mean saving our treasure,

Cap'n!' said the First Mate.

'Ah, we won't have saved it till we catch those scallywags,' said the Cap'n. 'All hands, prepare to make sail!'

Molly and I ran up the rigging, and soon The Saucy Sally was in full sail. She's a fine, fast little craft, and she flies over the waves when she's running before the wind. There was a good, strong breeze, too.

'Whose turn be it to take the watch today?' said the Cap'n.

'Mine, Cap'n!' I said.

'Right, Jim lad,' he said. 'Do ye get aloft and keep a weather eye peeled for that villain Swagg. Strap me if we won't be catching up with that barnacled old tub of his soon enough!'

I scrambled up to the crow's nest, and scanned the horizon for any sign of a ship. There was nothing, although far

to the south I could see some dark
clouds.

The breeze kept up, and if anything,
it got stronger. Soon those black clouds
weren't so distant any more, either.
I kept searching the sea through my
spyglass, and just as I was about to give
up, I saw . . . a small black dot.

'Ship ahoy!' I called out.

'Be it Swagg, Jim lad?' the Cap'n
yelled from below.

'Too far to see . . . ' I yelled back. The
dot grew bigger and bigger, and soon

I could just about see the flag – the crossed cutlasses!

'There he be,' I shouted. ''Tis Cap'n Swagg!'

But even as I saw that it was him, The Sea Slug was blotted out by a huge, dark cloud. The wind was really howling now, and I knew we were running into a storm.

'Get ye down from there, Jim lad!' called the First Mate. 'We need ye here below!'

By the time I got down from the crow's nest, The Saucy Sally was pitching and rolling in heavy seas. Great waves crashed across the decks, and everything that wasn't lashed down was swept overboard.

'Take in the topsail!' roared the Cap'n, although we could hardly hear him over the sound of the gale. 'All

hands to the pumps! Batten the hatches!
Lay a-hold there!'

It was a terrible storm, and it seemed
to go on for hours. At last, the wind
began to drop, and the waves grew
smaller. Soon the sea was almost calm,
and the sun broke through the clouds.

And there before us was an island.

I knew straight away it was the place
we wanted. Rising from the sea was a
mountain with two big caves in its front,
separated by a line of trees. It looked

just like a skull, and must have given the
island its name.

'Let's be havin' a look at that there
map, Jim lad,' said the Cap'n. We
decided to land at the spot called Cut-
Throat Cove, which was round the
other side of the island. From the line
drawn on the map, it seemed to be the
best place to start our search for the
treasure.

'All hands prepare for action,' said the
Cap'n. 'That villain Swagg may well be

laying in wait for us, the treacherous dog!'

The First Mate steered us through some difficult reefs, and soon we were coming round the last headland before the cove. We edged round it slowly . . .

'There they be!' called Molly from the bow. 'There's The Sea Slug!'

'Stand by to attack!' called the Cap'n. But The Sea Slug was at anchor, and strangely quiet. Nothing happened. No cannon roared, and no Cap'n Swagg was to be seen on the poop deck. We pulled alongside.

'It do look like we're too late,' said the First Mate.

There on the beach nearby were footprints heading towards the mountain . . . and the treasure!

Chapter Five

In which Jim and Molly disobey orders

There were two sets of footprints. One of them was normal enough, but the other looked very peculiar. There was one footprint every so often, but on either side of it there were two small holes in the sand.

'That must be Bosun Billy,' said Molly. 'He hasn't got his peg leg, so he's using crutches.'

'Well spotted, Molly me lass,' said the First Mate.

'So Swagg and Bosun Billy are after the treasure, are they . . . ' said the Cap'n, rubbing his chin. 'Shiver me timbers! We'd better get after them, and right enough!'

'Can we come, too?' I asked.

'Ah, Jim lad,' said the Cap'n, 'someone's got to guard The Saucy Sally, and make sure the rascals don't double back and make off in The Sea Slug. So ye had better stay here, Jim and Molly, while the First Mate and me sort the villains out!'

'Oh, Cap'n,' we said together. 'That's not fair!'

'And what have I said to 'ee afore?' said the Cap'n. 'I do be the judge of what be fair.'

'But we never get to do anything exciting,' I said.

'Jim's right, Cap'n,' said Molly. 'We

always have to stay behind while you and the First Mate go off to do something interesting.'

'Orders is orders, Jim and Molly,' said the First Mate. 'But we won't be long, see if I don't be right!'

'And there be plenty of things to do while we're gone,' said the Cap'n. 'Ye can start by swabbing down the decks and checking all the rigging.'

There was nothing more to be said, so Molly and I watched while the Cap'n and the First Mate got ready. They loaded their pistols, picked up their cutlasses, and went off with the map. We waved until they disappeared into the jungle where it came down to meet the beach.

'Right,' said Molly. I could tell that she was feeling particularly bossy. 'I'm in charge. You do the swabbing, and I'll

keep watch just in case Cap'n Swagg comes back.'

'Why should I do it?' I said. 'And who says you're in charge? And anyway, I'm better at keeping watch than you are, so why don't *you* do the swabbing?'

Molly looked for a moment as if she were going to lose her temper. But then she smiled instead.

'I've got a much better idea,' she said. 'They told us we couldn't go with them . . . but they didn't say anything about staying on board The Saucy Sally. Why don't we see if we can find out anything by having a look round . . . The Sea Slug?'

I thought it was a terrific idea. We got out The Saucy Sally's dinghy, and rowed across to Cap'n Swagg's ship. There was a rope hanging down the side. Molly grabbed it and climbed up.

I followed her, and soon we were
standing at the same spot on the poop
deck where I'd first seen Cap'n Swagg
waving his hook at us.

The Sea Slug was about the same size
as The Saucy Sally, but we soon saw it
was a very different craft altogether. For
a start, it was very dirty and untidy. It
looked as if the decks hadn't been
swabbed for weeks, and there was loose
rigging hanging everywhere.

'Come on,' said Molly. 'Let's have a
look below decks.'

Molly went round a corner and into a dark passageway. I followed, but I couldn't see her anywhere. A door was half open, and I pushed it cautiously . . .

'Boo!'

I nearly jumped out of my skin. It was Molly, and she was laughing her head off.

'Whose cabin is this anyway?' I said, when Molly quietened down.

'It looks like old Swagg's,' she said. She opened a cupboard door and looked inside. 'Phew! It's just as dirty and untidy in here as it is everywhere else.'

Molly was right, and the untidiest part of the cabin was the chart table in the corner. I went over to it, and picked up one of the papers that was lying on top.

And when I read what it said, my heart stopped.

'Molly!' I said. 'Look at this! It's the plan of an ambush! Swagg and Bosun Billy are going to ambush the Cap'n and the First Mate!'

Molly looked at the piece of paper, and then at me.

'Swagg means to make sure he gets clean away with the treasure,' she said. We've got to warn them!'

We rushed up on deck, and I started down the rope towards our dinghy. Molly was about to follow, when she stopped.

'Hang on a minute,' she said. 'There's something I must do . . . '

She ran off, and I heard some strange banging noises. Then she came back, and we climbed down the rope. She said she didn't have time to explain what she'd done, and I thought no more about it.

Soon we were following the tracks up the beach and into the jungle. The jungle was very thick, and it was easy to find the path Cap'n Swagg and Bosun Billy, then the Cap'n and the First Mate, had cut through it. Half an hour after we'd left the beach, we reached a clearing.

'Ssh!' whispered Molly. 'Do you hear voices?'

I pushed back a big leaf carefully and looked towards where the sound was coming from.

There before us were the Cap'n and the First Mate, each lashed to a palm tree – with Cap'n Swagg and Bosun Billy standing over them, pistols in hand!

Chapter Six

In which X marks the spot!

Molly was all for rushing into the clearing then and there, but I held her back.

'They've got pistols, and we haven't,' I said. 'Let's wait and see.'

So we stayed hidden, and peered through the leaves. Cap'n Swagg was strolling up and down in front of the Cap'n and the First Mate. He was laughing and talking, and looked very pleased with himself.

'A brilliant ambush, though I do say so myself,' he was saying.

'I should have known a cowardly traitor like ye would play such a scurvy trick,' said the Cap'n.

'Ah, Bluebeard,' said Swagg, 'but it worked, did it not? And now I have the treasure, and ye have . . . nothing! But I must not be too hard on ye. If ye hadn't done all that digging, why poor Bosun Billy and myself would have had to get our hands dirty.'

So saying, Swagg walked over to a large iron-bound sea-chest that was standing by a big hole in the ground. There was a big lock, which he gripped and shook.

'Psst! Look, Molly,' I whispered. 'That must be the treasure . . . they got the Cap'n and the First Mate to dig it up for them!'

'Ye'll never get away with it, Swagg,' said the First Mate. 'And even if ye do, we'll come after 'ee!'

The smile on Swagg's face vanished.

'Ye won't be going anywhere, ye Bluebeards!' he said with a sneer. 'Ye'll be staying here, lashed fast! Come on, Billy. Let's be away with the treasure.'

'Aye aye, Cap'n Swagg!' said Bosun Billy. He kept the Cap'n and the First Mate covered while Swagg dragged the treasure chest into the jungle.

'Farewell, numbskulls!' he called, then he and Bosun Billy were gone.

Molly and I waited a few moments, just to make sure they didn't return, and then we burst into the clearing.

We untied the Cap'n and the First Mate, and then explained how we'd found out about the ambush and had come to warn them.

'What are we going to do about the treasure, Cap'n?' said Molly. 'We can still catch them if we hurry.'

'Let them go, Molly me lass,' he said with a smile. 'I'll wager they haven't got quite what they bargained for in that there treasure chest.'

Neither Molly nor I understood what he meant. It was the First Mate who explained.

'That there chest was buried by Cap'n Smiley,' she said, 'and I'll bet there's nothing in it. Old Smiley was a great one for practical jokes, and that's the surprise that was meant in the rhyme on the map. The real treasure's probably buried somewhere else. And all we've got to do is find it.'

So that was what the rhyme on the map was all about! But where could the real treasure be?

'Let's have a peep at that there map again, First Mate,' said the Cap'n. 'What do it say? "Find Cap'n Smiley's treasure chest . . . " Well, old Swagg's done that . . . "Then find the X, and you'll find the rest." Find the X, eh . . . we'd better split into search parties.'

We all went off separately and scoured the clearing. We were looking for anything that might be an X, a mark on the ground, crossed sticks, anything. I had no luck, and after a while I went to find the others.

They looked as if they'd given up, too. They were standing beneath the two trees the Cap'n and the First Mate had been lashed to.

As I walked towards them, I saw something that made me stop in my tracks. Those trees . . . that was it!

'Cap'n! First Mate! Molly!' I shouted.

Also in Young Puffin

MYSTERY AT MUSKET BAY

Tony Bradman

"Ghosts and graveyards! Ghosts and graveyards!"

Trelawney the parrot is certain Dead Man's Island is haunted. He won't stop squawking about it! But the rest of the Bluebeard family think there might be more to the mystery of Musket Bay when they find strange footprints in the sand. Would a real ghost leave footprints?

Also in Young Puffin

Peril at the Pirate School

Tony Bradman

Miss Prudence Proper was tall and bony, and she had a big hooked nose. There were a couple of hairy warts right on the end of it. Some of her teeth were missing, some were green, and the rest were black.

Molly and Jim have been sent to Miss Prudence Proper's Academy for Pirate Pupils. But even for a pirate school, the teachers are very strange. Soon Jim is in deadly danger. Can Molly save him? What is *really* happening at the school?

GUNS OF WRATH

Colin Bainbridge

Will Comfort's burning mission — to wreak vengeance on the man who had him incarcerated during the Civil War — brings him to the town of Cayuse Landing. There, as he becomes drawn into the conflict between ruthless rancher Rank Wilder and the local townsfolk, he must question who really is his enemy. Women from his past and present are caught up, and he's not alone in having to face up to his loyalties and beliefs amidst escalating violence . . .

BREAKOUT

Greg Mitchell

Mickey Dole's gang breaks out of jail, killing and plundering in their bid for freedom. Ranch hand Clem Shaw joins a posse that includes a devious bounty hunter and a reluctant lawman. As the hunt progresses, he realizes that things are not at all clear-cut: his enemies are not all in the fugitive gang — which is now divided amongst itself. Before he can unravel the puzzle, Clem faces more deaths, shootouts — and being on the wrong end of a gun . . .

HIT 'EM HARD!

Arizona Territory, 1882. The Apaches are running rings around the army, raiding, robbing and killing. Captain Nathan Kelso knows they must be confronted on their own terms, hitting fast and hard. But who'd listen to a washed-up, borderline drunk? However, he receives orders to form Company C, a light, mobile unit, dedicated to bracing the Apaches wherever they find them. And after its first mission, deep in Indian country, things just get even tougher for Kelso and Company C.

BEN BRIDGES

HIT 'EM HARD!

Complete and Unabridged

LINFORD
Leicester

First published in Great Britain in 2012

First Linford Edition
published 2013

*A catalogue record for this book is available
from the British Library.*

ISBN 978–1–4448–1561–0

Published by
F. A. Thorpe (Publishing)
Anstey, Leicestershire

Set by Words & Graphics Ltd.
Anstey, Leicestershire
Printed and bound in Great Britain by
T. J. International Ltd., Padstow, Cornwall

This book is printed on acid-free paper

This book was always going to be for Steve Hayes

1

It was a day like any other for stagecoach driver Frank Stamp — until an Apache arrow tore right through his neck. As the chipped-flint head skewered him he made a deep, choking sound and slumped sideways against his shotgun guard, Sam Walker.

It was a moment before Sam, who'd been dozing up on the Concord's high seat, realized exactly what had happened. Then, seeing the arrowhead at the end of the distinctive red shaft and feeling the warm spatter of blood that exited with it, shock hit him like a rabbit punch.

They were under attack by Indians!

As instinct took over he dropped his ten-gauge side-by-side Remington shotgun, shouldered the driver off him and grabbed for the ribbons that were even now slipping through the dead man's fingers. The driver fell lifelessly toward the far edge of the box and with a cry of 'Nooo!' Sam tried to stop him from tumbling right over the edge.

He was too late.

Frank Stamp dropped off the high seat to roll loosely among the creosote and beavertail that lined the trail.

Face screwed out of shape, Sam drew the reins to him, flipped an urgent shiver through them and bellowed at the six-horse team to pull harder. The stagecoach immediately lurched as its speed increased, but in Sam's inexpert hands it also began to yaw dangerously from left to right across the trail, slowly but surely losing its center of balance.

'Driver! *Driver!* What's happening up there?'

Sam didn't hear the question at first. He was too busy trying to focus on just getting them the hell out of there and not tipping the one-and-a-quarter-ton stage over in the process.

Still in shock, he was also thinking about Frank. *Frank* . . . Dammit, they'd known each other for years. It was almost impossible to think that Frank had just been killed in less time than it takes to blink, and that Sam would neither see nor talk to him ever again —

'*Driver!*'

At last the voice penetrated. Sam leaned a little to one side, threw a hurried glance back along the bowed side of the coach. A slightly-built, sad-looking man in his early forties, wearing a cheap gray suit and a lighter gray muley hat, was leaning out of the window, an alarmed expression turned up toward him. He was a printer by trade, Sam recollected vaguely, name of . . . Cranford? No . . . Crawford — Addison Crawford. He was travelling with his two young sons to see relations in Fortuna.

'What's happening?' called Crawford.

Sam opened his whiskery mouth to yell an answer, but the words dried abruptly in his throat — because it was just then that the Apaches broke cover.

They came boiling up out of a

brush-hidden wash not far to the north, about fifteen of 'em, astride nimble-footed, spotted ponies. They curved gracefully out onto the trail behind the coach and quickly began to catch up.

Sam's eyelids peeled back in alarm. '*Apaches!*' he yelled.

The coach hit a rut and pitched forward and back on its leather thoroughbraces, almost throwing him from the box. Above the rumble and roll of the lumbering coach, the constant *thrub* of horse-hooves, the frightened squeals of the two lady passengers and the clink and jingle of harness, he suddenly heard the high, excited *ki-yi-yis* of the Apaches and chanced another look over his shoulder.

His blood congealed.

The Apaches, following the coach in a fluid, racing knot, were guiding their ponies with knee-pressure alone, so as to leave their hands free to fire their captured carbines or loose more arrows from their short, ironwood bows.

Sam cursed as arrows *thwhipped*

through the air around him, knowing with demoralizing certainty that they weren't going to get out of this. They were still too far from Fortuna. And he couldn't drive the damn coach and protect it at the same time, it just wasn't possible —

There came the sudden, welcome snap of a handgun, and again Sam twisted around. He saw that the scrawny printer had produced a Colt from somewhere, and was doing his best, God bless him, to discourage pursuit.

More by accident than design, his first shot hit one of the lead ponies midway 'twixt cheek and its shoulder. The animal folded forward and plowed into the dust, hurling its rider forward over its head. The Apache hit the ground badly, snapped an arm and maybe both legs, and even though his companions tried to avoid him, he was dragged several yards beneath the hooves of at least two of the following animals.

5

Sam hoped it would discourage their pursuers.

It didn't.

Desperately he slapped at his team-animals. '*Git up there, you bastards! Git UP there!*'

He caught motion from the corner of his left eye and twisted his head that way. One of the Apaches had surged out ahead of the rest and was even now drawing level with the box, his horse going flat-out beneath him.

As the coach continued to sway drunkenly across the cactus-choked wilderness, Sam looked right into the Indian's broad, coppery face. The Apache was all fired-up, his eyes bright with blood-lust, his skin painted in the reds, blacks and whites of war.

His face became a grotesque mask as he screamed some sort of war cry and tried to aim his stolen carbine one-handed.

Flame spat from the Winchester's barrel and Sam's guts tightened even as his bowels threatened to loosen, but the

6

bullet went wide.

With a frustrated roar the Apache tried to work the lever with a single, savage jerk of his right arm. While he was doing that, Sam looked around for his shotgun. In his haste to snatch the reins before they left Frank Stamp's hands he'd dropped it and it had fallen to the floor of the box and thence into the shadows beneath the seat, alongside the strongbox they were carrying to Fortuna.

The Apache, meanwhile, had fumbled his first attempt to jack a fresh round into the Winchester and had to jerk his arm to work the lever again. It bought Sam just enough time to transfer the reins to his left hand and use his right to grab the only other weapon handy — Frank Stamp's twenty-foot bullwhip.

He closed his callused fingers around the stiff, twelve-inch handle, yanked the braided whip from its socket and brought his arm back and forward in one smooth motion. The whip snaked out to its full length, snapped like an angry turtle and then flew back through the air. The popper in which it ended — a single piece of leather dang'-near three feet long — slapped the Apache right in the face and he screamed and toppled backwards out of his saddle.

Sam had a sneaking suspicion that he might have taken one of the sumbitch's eyes out.

He *hoped* so.

But while Sam had been concentrating on the Apache to his left, another had come racing up on his right.

Now the Indian leapt from his horse onto the side of the coach and quickly scrambled up onto the roof.

Inside the coach, Addison Crawford immediately aimed his Colt at the ceiling and fired a shot at where he hoped the brave would be. It smacked into the roof but all the stacked baggage there stopped it from finding its target.

Sam heard a sound behind him, turned with fear shrinking his weathered skin, saw that his worst suspicion had become fact —

The Apache brought a buffalo jawbone club straight down on his head.

The blow had every ounce of the stocky Indian's strength behind it. The jawbone, its striking edge honed to razor sharpness, carved through Sam's high-crowned hat and shattered his skull. As Sam slumped dead but still quivering, the whip dropped from his left hand and the reins began to slip from his right.

The Apache quickly hopped down into the box and snatched for the reins.

He was too late.

They slipped over the edge of the box and fell between the traces, where they whipped and flipped and then tangled themselves around the wagon-tongue.

Behind him, Crawford fired another shot into the roof, unaware that the Apache was already in the box, shoving Sam Walker's corpse aside and wondering how in hell he was going to bring the coach to a halt.

Then he spotted the brake handle

and, grinning, set his foot hard against it.

Big mistake.

As he stamped on the brake the rear wheels locked. But because the coach was still going at full speed it immediately started fishtailing even more wildly than before. It rocked first onto its two left-side wheels, then slammed back down and over onto the two right-side ones, almost throwing the Apache from his perch.

The six-horse team, terrified by what was happening behind it, kept leaning into the traces, frantically dragging the wheel-locked coach along, and still it kept lurching from side to side, first left, then right, then left, then —

At last it tipped too far to recover its balance. The right-side wheel-spokes fragmented beneath the full weight of the coach and then the coach itself flipped over and smashed hard onto its side, flinging the Apache from the box. The vehicle spun around, hurling baggage in every direction, and turned over again as it dropped into a shallow wash, where it finally came to a bone-jarring halt on its starboard side.

Long before that happened, the wagon-tongue splintered and, suddenly free, the team-horses kept running.

At once several Apaches went after them, because out here good horseflesh was worth its weight in gold nuggets. But the remainder drew rein, leapt from their blanket saddles and, following their leader — a stocky, bow-legged older man with a distinctive steel-gray streak of hair running back from his forehead — hurried to surround the overturned coach.

At first the silence was almost total. Dust drifted sluggishly in the sticky afternoon air.

Then, from inside the coach there came the sound of a man groaning, of a woman sobbing, and a boy screaming in abject terror, '*Pa!*'

The Apaches exchanged grins.

One of them, a youngish brave with visible ribs and a washboard stomach, climbed eagerly up onto the coach and peered into the stuffy interior.

Almost immediately a gun-blast tore up from inside the coach and the Apache flew backward, his head lost in an explosion of blood, bone and hair.

Surprise laced with anger ran through the other Apaches. One of them, a chunkier man with a milk-white left eye, howled the dead brave's name: '*Hridayesh!*'

Then he took his late companion's place, stabbed a long-barreled Navy .36 into the coach and, without aiming, fired a single, booming shot.

Following hard on the action, he tore open the blood-spattered door and dropped down among the crazy spill of dead or dying passengers.

With relish, he set about finishing the job.

2

Riding slump-shouldered at the head of his strung-out ten-man patrol, Captain Nathan Kelso suddenly twitched out of the stupor into which he had fallen and raised his right hand. The blue-clad soldiers behind him reined to an untidy halt.

'Problem, Cap'n?'

Kelso glanced around as his sergeant, Mordecai Shannon, reined up along-side. The captain was a prematurely tired-looking man in his middle twenties, tall and lean beneath his sweat-darkened five-button pullover uniform shirt and tan canvas trousers.

In answer to the sergeant's question, he cut his bloodshot hazel-green gaze off across the quivering desert, which was bordered at its farthest edges by a line of jagged pale blue peaks, each one rising sharp toward the coppery sky above. 'Thought I heard something,' he replied. His sun-burnished face was narrow, with a badly-shaved but well-defined jaw above a strong neck. 'Sounded like gunfire.'

Shannon crossed callused hands over the pommel of his equipment-hung McClellan saddle. He, like all of them, was powdered with fine yellow dust, his face heat-flushed and sweat-run. 'Sure you didn't just imagine it, Cap'n?'

For just a moment anger flared in Kelso. He knew all too well Shannon's low opinion of him. But maybe the sergeant was right. They'd been raising so much noise as they quartered this section of the border country that he might well have been mistaken. Hell, he might even have dozed off and simply dreamt it. But out here you never took anything for granted, not if you wanted to keep breathing.

'I'm not sure,' he admitted at last. 'But let's go find out.'

Following his lead, the patrol broke into a dust-raising gallop toward the nearest patch of high ground, a low hill half a mile distant.

As the ground rose beneath them, the horses labored up across a slope stippled with yellow Mexican goldpoppies and around tall, skyward-lifting saguaros and occasional stunted velvet mesquites. When they were close to the ridge Kelso gestured that they should slow to a halt.

He dismounted even before his horse had stopped, and staggered a little. He dragged his field glasses from one saddle bag, then jogged the rest of the way to the summit with his thirty-eight inch saber knocking against his left leg.

He felt lousy; unquestionably the result of too much whiskey and too little sleep. As a consequence, the morning's patrol had been hard on him and as the heat had sweated the last of the alcohol out of his system he'd felt himself growing increasingly shaky.

When he reached the ridge he went down, swept off his black folding campaign hat to reveal the thick, curly blue-black hair beneath and then carefully surveyed the country beyond.

The big, arrow-studded Concord stagecoach that lay on its side in a wash a quarter-mile away stood out like a cowman in a convent. A turkey vulture was perched on the closed, skyward-facing door, its shaggy wings folded back and its head cocked inquisitively as it tried to figure out how to get to the feast inside.

Placing the field glasses to his eyes, Kelso swept the desert from left to right. In short order he spotted what appeared to be a dead white man back along the trail a-ways, hatless, his skull a gleaming red mess.

A considerable way beyond the body lay a dead spotted horse, its legs a messy tangle, its body fairly heaving with greedy flies.

Kelso grimaced, swallowed softly, suddenly felt the need for a drink worse than ever.

When he was satisfied that the Apaches themselves were no longer in the vicinity, he loped back down to his horse. Watching him come, Shannon raised one heavy eyebrow questioningly. He was a big, moonfaced top kick of several years' standing, with perceptive blue eyes, a prominent, pitted nose and a lantern jaw. He was forty and looked every second of it, but he knew this country and the Indians who inhabited it practically better than any man Kelso had ever known, even though he in turn despised Kelso for what Kelso had become.

'Looks like the Apaches've hit the noon stage to Fortuna,' Kelso said grimly as he toed in and swung astride.

Shannon spat. 'Damn.'

Kelso made no reply, but *damn* just about summed it up.

He got them moving again, up over the ridge and down the far side toward the remains of the coach.

The turkey vulture saw them coming and flew away with a snap of shaggy wings. When they reached the coach, Kelso reined in and once again dismounted a little unsteadily. Behind him, the men automatically dragged their Springfield .45/.70s from the loops attached to their rear girth straps, their eyes everywhere at once.

Wordlessly Kelso, Shannon and a trooper named Lane Carr, a one-time veterinarian who was now the closest thing they had to a medic, approached the coach. The blood that still glistened wetly on the sky-facing door made the air smell like copper.

Carr, a thin, fair, freckled man of about thirty, clambered up the underside of the coach and peered inside. This close, they could all hear the busy drone of the flies inside.

'Aw golly,' muttered Carr.

Kelso looked up at him, eyes narrowed against the harsh sunlight. 'What have we got?' he asked.

Carr swallowed. 'Two men . . . two women . . . all dead, by the looks.'

Keeping his expression neutral, Kelso only nodded. Then: 'All right. Have a couple men give you a hand to get them out of there and see that they're wrapped in blankets ready for transportation back to the fort.'

'Yo!' Carr looked around. 'Baranski, Fitch! Come and give me a hand here!'

While Carr went to work, the captain turned away, surveyed the surrounding desert and wondered who they were, these people about whom he'd just spoken so dispassionately. What were their names, their ages, their reasons for taking what had turned out to be such an ill-fated journey?

He'd likely never know, and in truth it didn't really matter. He'd deliver them to the funeral parlor in Ocotillo Creek, the town that had grown up just outside Fort Whitethorn, and there they'd be embalmed and left to rest in an ice-house until their next of kin could come get them or request that they be buried in the local cemetery.

All at once he felt tired beyond words. To a point he had sympathy for the Apaches. Over the years, they'd been pushed to the limit. In the beginning, the depredations of a few had been blamed on the many, and following the Camp Grant Massacre back in '71, when the so-called 'Tucson Committee of Public Safety' had attacked Chief Eskiminzin's peaceful village at San Carlos and killed every man, woman and child there, Lieutenant-Colonel George Crook had been sent to make amends and broker some kind of peace before the situation degenerated beyond all salvation.

The peace had called for the Apaches to swap their hitherto-free, nomadic life for a static, more regimented existence on the reservation at San Carlos. It was an option many took. It was also one that many more rejected.

And who could blame them? At San Carlos the Apaches knew they'd be crammed into a reservation where disease was rife. They'd be half-starved by a combination of greedy Indian agents who deliberately withheld supplies, and a genuine difficulty in getting those same supplies to them in the first place. Hunter-gatherers by tradition, they'd be forced instead to farm the land, even though the blistering heat and pitiful lack of water meant that farming that chunk of northern Arizona was next to impossible.

Crook — whom the Apaches had respectfully named *Nantan Lupan,* or 'Gray Wolf' — had been ordered to hound and capture those co-called 'hold-outs' who refused to surrender to reservation life, and reluctantly he had done exactly that. He'd tracked them down in the Tonto Basin, the Mazatal Mountains, at Turret Peak and beyond, and from this crusade had emerged two of the most notorious hold-outs of them all — Geronimo and Victorio.

These two had introduced a new form of warfare to the conflict, that of hit-and-run. Victorio had been trapped and killed just two years earlier, but Geronimo was still out there, and so were various other bands of renegades, still hitting and running; the Chiricahua and the Mescalero, the Mimbreño and the Mogollon, the Arivaipa, Coyotero, Faraone Gileno and others . . . and sometimes Kelso didn't think there was a single damn' thing he or anyone else in this man's army could do to resolve the matter.

He heard Shannon rooting about in the stagecoach box and turned just as the sergeant spotted what he'd been looking for and went across to it; a small, sturdy strongbox which had been discarded several yards away, its lock broken, its dented lid thrown back.

The box was empty.

'What do you make of that?' Shannon asked as Kelso came over to join him. ''Paches got no use for money nor gold.'

'Maybe not,' said Kelso. 'But *white* men do.'

Shannon nudged his size six kepi back off his heavy brow. 'You sayin' it was *white* men did this?' he asked skeptically. His words said one thing, but his tone said something else: *Christ, you* must *be drunk.*

Before Kelso could reply, Trooper Carr shouted, '*Captain!* Come quick! One of these men is still alive!'

Clasping his saber by the hilt, Kelso crossed the trail at a dusty run.

Under instruction from Carr, Troopers Baranski and Fitch, the brawniest men in the patrol, had just set a slender-looking man in a rumpled gray suit down in the shade of the overturned coach. Now Fitch knelt beside the man, held a canteen to his mouth and helped him drink.

The man had a bookish look to him, with short, dark-blond hair, a thick moustache of the same color and incredibly sad blue eyes. He was, Kelso judged, about forty or so.

'As we take hold of him, he give moan,' explained black-bearded Baranski, his accent still thick with his Ukrainian origins.

'Till then we thought he was dead,' added Fitch.

It was, Kelso thought, an easy

mistake to have made. The poor fellow looked more dead than alive. His time-worn face was covered in the blood that had spilled from the deep gash in his forehead; this and the fact that he'd fallen deeply unconscious had probably convinced the Apaches he was dead, too, and inadvertently saved his life.

'You're all right now,' said Kelso, reaching out to squeeze the man's bony shoulder. 'What do they call you, mister?'

'C . . . Crawford . . . ' the wounded man said vaguely, fighting tears as he tried to get up. 'A . . . Addison Crawford.'

Kelso gently restrained him. 'It's okay now,' he said. 'What happened here, Mr. Crawford? Can you tell us?'

But Crawford shook his head urgently. 'You don't . . . *understand*,' he managed at last, his voice a dry croak. 'Wh-where are . . . where are my boys?'

Kelso's skin tightened uneasily. 'What was that?'

'My sons,' the other man said urgently, and his face seemed to crumple in the shadows of the body-littered, overturned coach. 'Wh ... where *are* they?'

'There were only four people in the coach, Mr. Crawford.'

'N-no ... ' wailed Crawford. 'Th-they were with me. J-Joseph and ... Ira. W ... we were going to F-F-Fortuna ... we have ... people there.'

Kelso glanced over his shoulder at Shannon. Shannon shook his head; no children had been found in or around the wreck.

'How old are they, Mr. Crawford?' Kelso asked.

'Seven ... seven and n-nine,' said Crawford. 'M ... maybe they wandered off ... '

'Maybe they did, at that,' Kelso agreed, but he didn't think so.

For a start, two boys that young wouldn't have gotten very far, especially after having been knocked around in

25

the stagecoach crash. He'd have been bound to see them from higher ground, through his field-glasses. And since the Apaches must surely have seen them when they finished off the other passengers, that left only one possibility.

'But I think it more likely that the Indians took them with them,' he said softly.

Crawford froze, his anguished blue eyes burning into Kelso's face. 'No!' he breathed.

But the more Kelso thought about it, the more likely it seemed. It was by no means unusual for the Apaches to take prisoners, especially children. Sometimes they kept them to bolster their own waning numbers, sometimes they figured to ransom them back to their families, sometimes they even traded them to the Comanches.

Crawford started struggling again, determined to rise and go after them. As weak as he was, it took all of Kelso's strength to hold him back.

'Let me . . . *go,* damn you!' Crawford

26

snapped. 'I have to . . . find my boys! They need me!'

'We'll bring your boys back, Mr. Crawford,' Kelso promised grimly.

But Crawford didn't even hear him. 'I've got to go after my boys!' he insisted, sobbing.

Abruptly Kelso tightened his grip to get the man's attention. Crawford looked at him, the whites of his eyes looking extra white against the blood that had now dried to a rusty crust on his brow and cheeks.

'Leave that to us, Mr. Crawford,' Kelso said more firmly. '*We'll* get your boys back.'

Crawford looked up at him, his eyes searching Kelso's face, desperate to believe that he could, and would.

'My word on it,' Kelso said gently.

That did the trick. Crawford slumped back, suddenly weak beyond belief.

Kelso, by contrast, powered back to his feet, suddenly filled with energy. 'Carr — patch this man up as best you can. Then you, Baranski and Fitch get

27

the rest of those people out of there and take 'em back to the fort. Rest of you men, get ready to ride! The Apaches took two white boys with 'em — and we're going to get 'em back!'

3

At the Lolotea Apache Indian Reservation twenty miles north of Ocotillo Creek, Eli Gardner looked down at the young Apache girl perched warily on the edge of his narrow bunk and felt the breath hitch in his throat. She was about fourteen years old, tall and a little on the skinny side . . . but that was just how he liked them.

'Now,' he said carefully in his labored pidgin Apache. 'How 'bout a little smile for old Eli, huh?'

The girl looked up at him from beneath fine, lowered brows. Her name was Liluye, and though she was trying not to let it show, he knew she was terrified of him. She wore a simple fringed buckskin dress and deer-hide moccasins. Both had seen better days. Her black hair was center-parted and fell thick to her shoulders. Her close-set eyes were the color of coffee, her nose small and straight, her mouth wide and sober, her delicate chin pitted with what Gardner had come to think of as just the cutest little dimple.

Now he reached for the bottle of *tiswin* on the cabinet beside his striped, stained pillow and took a pull at the corn-based beverage. It was warm and slightly bitter and it made him shudder a little. Then, moving slowly so's not to spook her, he sat down next to her and carefully put one arm around her shoulders.

She stiffened beneath his touch, wanting to obey her natural instinct to rise and run, but knowing better.

Good, he thought. She could play the innocent if she liked, but she knew what was going to happen here this afternoon just as well as he did, and if she knew what was good for her she was going to play along like a good little squaw.

'That's a girl,' Eli said approvingly.

Embarrassed, she looked around the mean little room, anywhere but at him.

Gardner's cramped living quarters doubled as an inventory room and it was crowded with boxes of pressed soap and bolts of gaily-colored cloth. His narrow bunk ran along one wall, and an old chair sat to one side of a black, cast-iron stove. It was a miserable, cluttered mess of a place, home to sacks of beans and pungent pepper, dried fruit and cheap coffee, plug tobacco, a cracker barrel filled to the brim with stale crackers and two cases stuffed with dusty bottles of Balm of Childhood. But it was from here that he ran what he liked to think of as his empire, the Lolotea Reservation.

Gardner was the Reservation's duly-appointed Indian Agent, and since he was mostly left by the Bureau of Indian Affairs to get on with it, he enjoyed to the full the power he wielded over these heathens.

Though San Carlos was the best-known of Arizona's Apache reservations, there were almost a score of them scattered throughout the Territory. Here, as on most of the smaller ones, trouble was almost unheard-of. The Apaches who lived here had been whupped good by the Army. Their spirits had been broken, and even now they lived in fear of reprisal should one of their number ever step out of line.

Gardner, a gangly, underfed man of forty-six summers, whose pale face was all skull and whiskers, encouraged that fear. Outwardly he pretended to be concerned for the Apaches' welfare, and constantly counseled them not to make trouble lest they incur the wrath of the Great White Father, who was, he said, a close personal friend. Inwardly, however, he exploited them . . . *some* of them, at least.

And it wasn't exactly difficult. The Apaches lived by what they called *customs*. Their philosophy was simple. If you violated those customs you would be punished. If you obeyed them, then all remained well. Thus, it followed that if they obeyed the customs as set down by Agent Eli

Gardner, they'd get by.

'Now,' he said, his voice lowering even as his heart-rate picked up expectantly, 'I'm gonna say this one more time, so we both know where we stand, you got it?'

The girl hesitated briefly, then nodded.

'It's a hard life, lookin' after you people,' he said. 'An' the B.I.A. makes it a damn' sight harder. Paperwork . . . red tape. Red *tape* for red *skins*, huh?'

He chuckled, revealing long, gappy teeth the color of unbleached linen.

'I do what I can for you-all,' he went on when it became clear that she had failed to see the humor in his jest. 'But still you folks go to bed at night hungry. I bet *you* go to bed hungry, don't you, Liluye?'

The girl nodded hesitantly.

'Well, that pains me, child, it surely does. Pains me that a fine man like your pa, and your mama and brothers and sisters, they all go to bed hungry, too. But the thing about me, Liluye, is this. I

33

make a powerful enemy, but I can also make a good friend. A damn good friend. See what I'm sayin', child?'

She continued to look at him, her eyes now unreadable.

'You be good to *me*,' he said softly, 'and I'll be good to *you*. Make sure you and your folks never go hungry again.'

Again she looked away from him, inspecting the dim room, with its moldering square of cloth yanked carelessly across the single window, with clear distaste.

Gardner watched her for a moment, then said, 'It's a lonely life out here, girl. I got no woman, no folks to speak of. Just me. And *you*.' He closed his fingers around her shoulder and squeezed, almost savoring the shiver that trickled through her.

'So it's in the nature of what you might call a business arrangement,' he went on, more briskly. 'You let me . . . *enjoy* your comp'ny . . . and I'll see to it that your folks don't want for nothing.'

He smiled — until the smile suddenly vanished like a card up a magician's sleeve.

''Course, it'd have to be our secret,' he murmured sternly. 'It'd *have* to be. The Great White Father would be very angry if he thought you'd seduced me.'

Her eyes went round at that. 'This I would not do!' she protested. 'I only came here this afternoon because you told me to — '

Gardner's bony face turned hard. 'But it'd be your word against mine,' he reminded her. 'And who do you think the Great White Father'd be more likely to believe?'

He reached across and twisted her around so that he could look straight at her. He could only imagine the ripe young body beneath her dress . . . but if he was lucky, he wouldn't have to rely on imagination for too much longer.

'So, you an' me . . . we gonna have us a mutually *beneficial* relationship, child. 'Cause if we *don't*, I might just have to tell the Great White Father that you came in here and tried to take advantage of me.' He shook his head. 'You folks think you're hard done-by now, you wait till the Great White Father hears about *that.*'

'P-please . . . ' she said in a soft, scared voice.

Gardner understood the girl's reluctance. Unlike, say, the Navajo, the Apaches guarded their chastity well and did not surrender it lightly. But he'd watched this girl grow and blossom and knew that she was rapidly approaching the age and sexual maturity where she would be married off. Gardner had wanted to get her before that happened.

And now here she was.

She started crying, but didn't pull away from him. That was good, too, he told himself. Maybe she thought she could hide the fact that she'd been deflowered. Let her think that, anyway. But Gardner knew that it would become all too obvious on her wedding night, and then she'd pay for it. The choice would be stark; have her nose sliced off or be banished to the mescal grounds, there to dig pit-ovens and roast the hearts of the ninety-pound mescal plants she'd have to gather for the tribe, an outcast among her people.

'Come on, now,' he coaxed. 'Never know, child, you might actually *like* it.'

He drew her closer to him. He smelled of sweat and smoke and coffee, and instinctively now she *did* rebel, and try to push him away.

He usually liked it when they struggled, but he wasn't in the mood for it today. He wanted this girl, had wanted her for a long time, had waited as patiently as he knew how until the opportunity had presented itself so that he could catch her by herself and tell her to come see him, and not to tell anyone about it because the Great White Father wouldn't like that.

Now he figured he'd waited long enough.

His fingers closed on her, their tips digging into her flesh. She winced, continued to struggle against him, but pride forbade her from crying out for help, even supposing help could be had.

Heavier and stronger than she, it was just moments before he had her sprawled on the unmade bunk and he was on top of her, his lank, dusty black hair hanging around his now-flushed face.

His whiskery mouth tried to find hers. She twisted her head first one way, then the other, to avoid him.

This, he decided, was proving to be more difficult than he had expected. The girl clearly didn't understand that what was required here was a little cooperation.

She still needed teaching.

He pushed up on one elbow, brought his other hand up to strike her —

— and the door slammed open.

Before Gardner could climb off the girl someone grabbed him by the hair, twisted roughly and dragged him away from her. Pain burning through his scalp, Gardner's face twisted up and he stumbled to his feet.

'What the . . . what the hell — ?'

Before he could say more, he felt something sharp and cold kiss the skin at his hairline, and froze.

A blade.

Oh God no, no, the bastard's gonna scalp me —

He almost passed out with fear, but the man behind him twisted his fingers a little tighter in Gardner's hair and kept him upright.

'What's your name, child?' asked the man holding the blade to Gardner's hairline.

Gardner recognized the voice immediately. That slow, deep, rumble belonged to Lew Eden, a Seminole-Negro half-breed who worked as a scout at Fort Whitethorn . . . and a man he had always been leery of.

The girl rolled off the bunk, glad to get away from it. She stood with her head down, looking at the newcomer from beneath shame-lowered brows. 'Liluye,' she stammered after a while.

'All right,' said Eden, his tone

gentling suddenly. 'You can go on home now, Liluye.'

She stared up at him, unbelieving.

Thinking fast, Gardner said, 'Uh, yeah. Yeah, run along, Liluye.' And to Eden, still holding the blade oh-so-gently against his skin, 'Good child, that one, L-Lew. Helps out around here. You know, cooks for me sometimes, cleans up, helps around the store.'

The newcomer ignored him, instead concentrating on the girl. She looked up at him, still scared, uncertain. He smiled at her, gave a short nod, offered her a wink to let her know that everything was okay.

Deciding that indeed it was, Liluye allowed relief to wash across her face. Her shoulders sagged and she hurried for the splintered door, now dangling drunkenly from one hinge.

Gardner called desperately, 'Uh . . . thanks for helpin' out, Liluye. Don't ferget what I said about the Great White Father.'

The girl slipped away without a

40

backward glance and left the store at a run. After she was gone it grew very quiet in the cluttered room.

Then Lew Eden released his grip and shoved Gardner hard so that he twisted and landed with a bounce on the bunk.

He looked up at the man who had ended his fun with the girl.

Eden stood five feet ten and weighed a hundred and sixty pounds. He wore a high-crowned black hat with a flat brim, a brown bib shirt, black jeans tucked into high, straight boots. Around his hips he wore a thick shell-belt. A double-action Model 1878 .41-caliber revolver sat in the pocket against his right hip. Against his left lay a beaded sheath that usually carried the stone-headed hatchet he now held in one big, tough-knuckled fist; a hatchet whose cutting edge was always kept well-honed.

Gardner swallowed softly, but the sound came loud in the thick silence.

Lew stared down at him with clear contempt. The son of a runaway slave who had gone on to become a prominent Florida landowner and a brighter-than-average Seminole squaw, he was about thirty-five. Beneath his hat he wore his straight black hair short, with a left-hand part. His skin was the color of burnished copper, the brows over his dark, lidded eyes arched. He had a direct nose, high cheekbones, a strong chin, ears that sat flat to his skull.

Before coming north and west to the Arizona Territory he'd served with the Seminole-Negro Indian Scouts on the plains of southern Texas, where he'd fought Kiowa, Kiowa-Apache, Cheyenne, Arapaho and Comanche and somehow lived to tell about it. When the Indian Wars down there finally came to an end back in '75, he'd travelled north and seen action in the Great Sioux War.

Now Gardner studied the half-breed uneasily. 'L-Lew,' he said. 'What, uh . . . what brings you out this way?'

Lew eyed the agent for a moment

more. 'The Great White Father,' he muttered at last. 'Way I hear it, you an' President Arthur are bosom buddies.'

Gardner gestured nervously. 'I didn't even *vote* for the man.'

'Maybe you didn't. But the way you been tellin' it, you got the president's ear . . . an' if the folks around here don't do like you say, they'll feel the back of his *hand*.'

Gardner tried unsuccessfully to make a dismissive gesture. 'Oh, you d-don't want to pay no mind to talk like that! I only tell them that so they'll know who's boss around here an' toe the line.'

'It goes deeper than that, way I hear it,' Lew said bleakly. 'You use the Great White Father to scare these people into doing like you say. Especially the young girls.'

'Now see here — !'

'Nope,' said Eden, and the single word stopped Gardner's denial dead in its tracks. 'I thought they were rumors, at first, Eli. Didn't think even a scoundrel like you would stoop so low as to molest children. But it seems I was wrong.'

'Is . . . is that why you're here?' asked the Indian agent.

'In a manner of speakin',' said Eden. 'See, I know what's been goin' on around here, Eli, an' it makes me sick to my stomach. But it ends right *now*.'

'You . . . you can't *kill* me,' gasped Gardner, his eyes drawn again to the hatchet. 'I'm a Gov'mint employee! You . . . you kill me and there'll be hell to pay!'

Lew nodded. 'An' we don't want that, do we?' he said mildly. 'I mean, these here folks, the ones you been charged with lookin' after, they've had enough of hell. I kill you now, the B.I.A. comes in an' starts askin' questions. Questions that could bring shame on a lot of young girls who already feel ashamed enough about what you made them do.'

'So . . . ' Gardner licked his thin, dry lips. 'So what you gonna do, uh . . . Lew?'

'We're gonna make sure it doesn't happen again,' the half-breed said simply. 'Because from now on, it's *you* who's gonna toe the line, Eli. No more starvin' these people so you can sell what's rightfully theirs off to your cronies in Ocotillo Creek. No more taking advantage of girl-children. From now on, you're gonna be whiter'n white. And you know *why?*'

Gardner thought he did, but he still shook his head.

''Cause I'll be watchin' you from now on,' Lew promised grimly. 'Any talk that gets back to me about you that I don't like . . . '

He moved then, moved so fast that he was just a blur. The hatchet left his hand, spun end-over-end and slammed into the edge of the bunk between Gardner's legs, uncomfortably close to his recently-aroused manhood . . . which instantly shriveled still further.

'I make myself clear?' asked Lew.

Gardner muttered something.

'What was that again?' demanded the half-breed.

'*Yes!*' Gardner blurted. 'Yes, damn you! You make yourself clear!'

'Then you can start right away,' said Lew, stepping in close so that he could drag the hatchet free and slide it back into its sheath. 'By issuin' extra supplies to everyone.'

He turned and strode slowly back to the broken door, where he looked back over one slab-muscled shoulder. 'I *mean* it, Eli. Don't give me cause to come back this way,' he warned in a flat tone. 'If you *do,* you can kiss your John Thomas goodbye.'

It wasn't until Lew quit the store and Gardner was left all alone that he realized he'd wet himself.

4

It was heading toward dusk when Lew came within sight of Fort Whitethorn.

It had been a good afternoon, all things considered. He'd had his suspicions about Eli Gardner for a while now, but it had been hard work getting the Apaches at Lolotea to open up and tell him anything about just how the man was running the reservation.

Apaches were the most direct people in a stand-up fight, but in a conversation they tended to skirt around things. In this case, it was partly down to shame; they were ashamed to admit that they feared reprisals from the Great White Father if they didn't turn a blind eye and do as Gardner said. And it had taken a lot of straight-talking from Lew to convince them otherwise. But once he had . . .

It had been like watching a dam

burst: the stories, the suspicions, the truths about Gardner's sexual tastes that the beaten, broken Apaches had not wanted to admit even to themselves; everything had come out, and as it did so Lew Eden had listened with mounting fury.

But the matter was settled now. He felt he had taught Gardner a lesson he wouldn't forget any time soon, and that could only be to the benefit of the People, as the Apaches called themselves.

Further thought was interrupted just then by the sight of a slow-moving, strung-out patrol heading in off the scrubby flats to the south, and recognizing Nathan Kelso at its head, he heeled his horse to speed so that he could intercept them.

He and Kelso both understood that there were two sides to every disagreement, that no one side in this apparently endless war was entirely innocent, just as no one side was entirely guilty. Most army scouts had spent enough time among white man and red to understand this, but it was still relatively rare for a soldier to have any real understanding of his enemy, much less sympathy. Still, for all his faults, Kelso was such a man.

The sun was half-hidden behind the distant mountains as he cut a diagonal course across the plain to join the patrol. Its light bathed the desert in a million shades of amber, and dyed the long-stretched shadows a pleasant, powdery blue.

When he drew close enough, however, he read something in the weary, dispirited slump of Kelso and his men that made his smile of greeting vanish. ''Sarge,' he called across to Shannon. ''Cap.'

Kelso nodded distractedly. 'Lew.'

'Trouble?' asked Lew.

'Apaches hit the noon stage to Fortuna this afternoon,' Kelso replied. 'Hascha's band. Killed all but one of the passengers and crew and stole away a couple of boys.'

The last of Lew's previous good humor immediately evaporated.

The taking of prisoners had long been practiced by the Apaches. Children in particular were seen as the life-blood of the tribe, a guarantee of its continued existence. They were quickly indoctrinated into the ways of the People and either picked up the language and customs real quick or else faced regular beatings until they did. Once they were part of the tribe they were put to work tending livestock or hunting small game, which gave the braves more time and freedom to hunt, raid and defend their camps.

'What happened?' he asked.

'What do you think happened?' countered Kelso. 'We gave chase, but they had the beating of us — as usual.'

And even though he didn't want to, Kelso saw it all over again, in his mind.

They'd pushed their horses hard, hoping to cut the Apaches off before they could cross the border into Sonora, but by the time they saw their quarry's dust hanging on the horizon Kelso had known they were too late; Hascha's Apaches were already well over the line.

Even so, he was damned if he'd give up the chase so easily.

The border between the Arizona Territory and the Free and Sovereign State of Sonora was a blurred line that was neither Mexican nor American but an almost unique mixture of the two. But the border country ahead of them was peopled mostly by the Yaqui, Pima and Tohono O'odham, and if it came to it they'd side with the Apaches, and not take kindly to what they would see as an invasion by foreign forces.

Then there was the gray-and-silver-clad *Guardia Rural* to consider. Out here the *Rurales* usually patrolled in groups of thirty, and this far north such patrols were made up of the toughest men the Mexican police had to offer. A law unto themselves, they would engage any soldiers from the hated *Los Estados*

Unidos without hesitation, safe in the knowledge that they could justify any such action.

Kelso had known all that, but what was an exchange of gunfire — even a full-blown diplomatic incident, if it came to that — when weighed against the lives of Addison Crawford's two sons?

So he'd pushed on, even as the Apaches had widened the distance between them; even when he knew they couldn't hope to catch up.

Hascha had known it as well, had deliberately hauled rein and turned his pony around even as the rest of his band kept pushing south, and Kelso had been forced to watch through his field-glasses as the Apache waved his ancient musket back and forth over his head and screamed obscenities, taunting them, laughing at them.

And it *was* Hascha, for though Kelso had never seen the Apache before, the distinctive streak of silver-gray hair that swept back through his otherwise black mane identified him beyond all doubt.

That was when Sergeant Shannon had called his name, and hearing it, Kelso had turned to the moon-faced NCO. Shannon had looked him in the eye, shook his head, and his expression had said, *We can't go any further, Cap'n. We daren't.*

Kelso knew he was right, but that didn't make the decision any easier to make. What *did* was the sure and certain knowledge that even if they kept going, the Apaches — riding light on smaller horses bred for stamina and mobility — would sooner or later lose them in the vast, fertile valley of Sonora.

So Kelso had nodded, reined down, called a halt to the pursuit and even though he knew it was the right thing, the *only* thing, he could have done, still he hated himself for it.

Now, listening to the story, Lew Eden could only say, 'Too bad, Cap.'

Kelso looked at him. 'Yeah — too bad,' he growled sourly. 'Too bad we lose too damn' often against the likes of Hascha.'

Lew shrugged. 'You know why, Cap. You soldier-boys need to be as light an' mobile as he is.'

It was a conversation they'd had more than once in the past, and it had become a growing source of frustration to Kelso, especially today, when so much more had rested on them being able to catch up with the enemy.

They'd entered Ocotillo Creek's main street by this time, and some of the locals, having heard about the attack on the Fortuna stage from the men who'd brought in the bodies, came out to watch them pass by. Sight of them only made Kelso feel his failure to rescue Crawford's boys all the keener.

At the far end of Main stood Fort Whitethorn. Built along standard military lines, it was an orderly collection of low adobe buildings surrounded by a low, whitewashed stone wall. More of a military outpost than a fort, the regimental standard hung limp against a tall pole at the center of the parade ground, for the approaching evening was humid and still.

They rode tiredly through the gate. The company barracks, enlisted men's kitchen and mess hall had all been built along the eastern wall, with a modest infirmary, guardhouse and stable/corral facing it to the west. Officer's country — that was, the CO's quarters, adjutant and officers' quarters, kitchen and mess, plus married quarters — lay directly ahead, on the far side of the parade ground.

Around them, soldiers stopped what they were doing, singly or in groups, to watch the returning patrol.

As Kelso led his men toward the stables he saw a figure stumble out of the infirmary, his head wrapped in a bright white bandage. He knew who it was even before he properly focused on the man; Crawford, expecting to see his sons, destined to be disappointed.

Again Kelso's need for a drink surfaced with a vengeance. He'd been dreading this moment, but he turned his mount toward Crawford even as the other man came unsteadily across the parade toward him.

'My boys . . . ' he called. His voice, still weak, nevertheless carried across the distance and echoed faintly on the evening air. He craned his neck to get a better look at the patrol in the dusk-light, his skin almost the color of chalk. 'My boys, Captain . . . wh-where are they?'

Kelso drew rein and cleared his throat. 'I'm sorry, Mr. Crawford, but we — '

'Are they dead?' Crawford interrupted with something like a sob. 'They're *dead?*'

Thinking the man might pass out, Kelso quickly stepped down and went to catch him by one arm. 'No, they're not dead, but — '

'Then where are they?' asked Crawford. 'You said you'd get them back, Captain . . . you told me . . . ' And here it came, as Kelso had known it would:

'You gave me your *word*.'

Inwardly he cringed. Yes, he'd given his word, in an age when it was the most valuable thing a man had to give. And still he'd failed.

'We just couldn't keep up with them,' he said. 'They were across the border before — '

Abruptly Crawford shrugged out of his grip and stepped back a pace. '*What?*' he barked. '*What?* You were within sight of them and you let them *go?*'

'There wasn't much choice, Mr. Crawford,' Kelso said doggedly. 'Much as I hated to do it, I had to call off the chase or risk an international incident.'

Crawford shook his head, tears sparkling in his sad, sick-looking eyes. 'You gave me your *word*,' he said again.

'I know. And I'm sorry.'

But Crawford didn't even hear him. 'My wife died three years ago,' he murmured, speaking almost to himself. 'My boys . . . they're all I have *left*.'

His chin dropped to his chest and his shoulders started heaving.

The sound of his sobs was an awful thing there in the amber-lit parade-ground, with its long-slanting shadows.

*   *   *

Kelso didn't think he'd sleep much that night. He was right. Every time he closed his eyes he saw Crawford's face, worn down, worn *out*, knowing that he'd just lost everything that mattered to him; and all because of Kelso.

The captain sat in his cramped, night-dark quarters and sipped whiskey from a thumb-smeared glass. He didn't want to think about the fate that awaited Crawford's boys, but he couldn't help it.

It was frightening just how quickly white captives, especially children, could slip into the Indian way of life. He'd seen it before. At that age the mind was fresh and receptive to new ideas. And as much as Crawford's boys would try to cling to the past, eventually they'd become as much an Apache as Hascha himself.

And then . . . ?

Crawford's boys were seven and nine. Ten years from now, if this war was still going, they'd be raiding and killing their own kind . . . or else they'd be languishing on a reservation somewhere, broken shades of their former selves. It wasn't the kind of future any man could envision for his sons.

Kelso poured more whiskey and cursed it for not blunting the self-hatred that was fierce within him. He'd come west four years earlier, full of expectation and ambition for his military career. All that awaited him was an endless round of fruitless patrols, the discovery of one massacre-site after another, of chasing Apaches who always, *always*, had the beating of him.

It was not the glorious career he had expected to enjoy.

Out here there was only dust, and

heat, and sweat, and struggle. Oh yes, and disappointment, of course, not to mention loneliness. And so, somewhere along the way, he had turned to the bottle. The bottle had kept him company through those long, lonely nights. The bottle helped him forget the terrible sights the raiding Apaches left behind them . . .

The bottle.

And now what was left of the great Nathan Kelso? A wreck, that was all; a joke of a man whom nobody could hate more than he did himself.

Sometime after two in the morning he must have dozed off, because the next thing he knew someone was hammering at his door and the small, square window was already turning gold with the new dawn.

He sat up, winced as his back complained at the sudden movement, then lurched, whiskery and still half-drunk, to the door.

When he opened it, he found Shannon standing outside in the sharp dawn. Shannon's eyes immediately went to a spot beyond his shoulder, saw the empty bottle and glass on the table, and he couldn't help it, his lip curled in disgust.

'Sorry to trouble you, Cap'n . . . '

Kelso waved that aside. 'What time is it?'

'Almost five.'

Kelso nodded. At least he hadn't slept through *Reveille*, then, which was still thirty minutes away.

'What's the problem?'

He believed he knew the answer even before Shannon gave it. 'Crawford,' said the sergeant. 'He's gone.'

Kelso let his breath go in a hiss. 'To find his sons,' he guessed.

'Near as I can tell, he snuck out sometime after midnight, stole a horse from the livery in town and then lit out,' Shannon went on. 'Orderly over at the infirmary found his bed empty about twenty minutes ago and came to fetch me.'

Kelso thought fast — no mean feat

for a man whose brain was still fogged by alcohol. Crawford had a five-hour start . . . to what? Any fool could find the border and cross it, but what then? Had he thought to steal a gun along with that horse? Supplies? And just how in hell did he think he was going to find Hascha's encampment and rescue his boys with the odds so tightly stacked against him —

But he stopped right there. The answer to that was simple. Crawford was out of his mind with grief, desperate . . . and he wasn't thinking straight.

Kelso told himself they should have seen this coming and maybe the fact that he hadn't was something else that would weigh heavy on his conscience.

'Find Lew Eden,' he said. 'Tell him what's happened and to get Crawford back before he runs into trouble.'

Shannon nodded. 'Yo! And you, Cap'n?'

Again, the message beneath the

words: *Goin' back to the bottle, are you?*

'Me?' said Kelso, reaching a decision. 'I'm going to do something I should have done a long time ago.'

5

Addison Crawford reined in and surveyed his surroundings through raw, squinted eyes. He didn't have a clue where he was. Oh, he'd been careful to keep the rising sun on his left, so he knew he was riding south . . . but where was the border? Had he already crossed it? And once he was in Sonora, then what?

He was thirsty, his head was throbbing worse than ever and he felt just about as close to rock bottom as it was close enough to get. Dr. Sutton, the army surgeon at Whitethorn, had meant well, telling him to rest and regain his strength. But how could he rest, with Joseph and Ira out there, captives of the Indians?

Were *they* resting right now? Of course they weren't! They were pining for the father they, like the Apaches, believed dead, and wondering what the uncertain future held for them and whether or not anyone even knew what had become of them.

So there could be no rest for Crawford, not yet.

But he had played it canny. He'd pretended to go along with Sutton and all the while he'd planned what he would *really* do, as soon as the chance presented itself.

He'd escaped.

Well, maybe *escape* was the wrong word. They'd left him alone in a small room at the end of the open ward, perhaps out of respect for his loss, and he'd waited until full dark and then he'd simply climbed out of the bed they'd put him in, hurriedly tucked a clean white shirt into his rumpled gray suit trousers, slipped into his elasticized Congress shoes and then gathered up his jacket, after which he stole off into the starry dark.

He was, of course, still weak, and the world continued to roll and lurch

65

around him. He had to stop once, close his eyes, wait for a cold sweat to run its course and his heart to stop its frantic thumping. Then, still keeping to the shadows, he left the fort behind him.

No one raised any alarm.

At Ocotillo Creek's only livery he stole a horse, and a saddle from the tree at the back of the big barn. He saddled up mostly by feel, taking his time because it wasn't something he'd ever had much call to do before. Then he'd walked the horse out beyond the town limits, mounted up . . . and rode.

He rode south, guided by the fact that the moon, because it had risen before the sun had fully set, was lit to the west. Even so, he veered off-course at least twice and had to correct himself as best he could with the dawn.

Around him now the wrinkled land was choked with drab, brittle-looking brush. But the further south he rode, the more lush the vegetation became. He took this as a good sign, because he had always been a voracious reader and remembered reading somewhere that the valley of Sonora was well-watered.

But with the rising sun came the building heat. It hammered at his back and shoulders and squeezed every last drop of moisture out of him. His headache grew worse and he realized with a sinking feeling that he hadn't even thought to fetch a canteen.

Still, there must be water around here somewhere. All he had to do was find it. But when he looked out at the shimmering plain, he saw for the first time just how vast and seemingly empty it really was. There was water here, of course there was . . . but a man would have to search hard to find it, and that would take time — time Crawford didn't believe he could spare.

So, stubbornly, he pushed on.

The new day grew hotter. He wore no hat; his only protection from the sun was the bandage still wrapped around his head. After a time he felt as if he was being cooked.

He slipped into a doze and woke

67

again with a start some indeterminate time later. The pounding in his head was sickening. He realized he had veered off-course again and despair engulfed him. He leaned sideways and dry-heaved.

Concentration was now difficult if not impossible. He felt completely, utterly bewildered.

He had no memory of passing out. No memory of sliding from the saddle and landing loosely in the shadow of his horse.

And no awareness of the three Apaches who suddenly rose up out of cover and, overcome with curiosity, slowly led their ponies closer.

★   ★   ★

Kelso entered the adjutant's office and said, 'I want to see Major Hackett.'

The adjutant, First Lieutenant Miller, had been sorting through the top drawer of a chunky wooden file cabinet. Now he turned, studied Kelso for a moment and said, 'The major's busy right now.'

There was nothing in Miller's manner that acknowledged Kelso's rank. Kelso was a joke around here, and the hell of it was, Kelso couldn't deny it. 'This won't take a minute,' he said stubbornly.

Miller elbowed the drawer shut. He was a good-looking young man with thick brown hair that was always immaculately barbered. He said, 'Wait a moment.'

He crossed the neat little ante-room, rapped knuckles against a door in the back wall and then went through to the office beyond.

Left alone, Kelso sagged a little. How could he have sunk this low? An army career was just about the only thing he'd ever wanted. And yet because it had failed to match his expectations, because he'd been sent to this little backwater where the best he could ever hope to do was clean up after the Apaches and the occasional border-crossing Mexican bandits had done their worst, he'd just given up.

The door opened again and Miller said, 'You can go in. But you'd better make it quick.'

Kelso brushed past him and into a small but tidy office. A Colonial model stove sat in one corner, its thin chimney disappearing through a hole in the low ceiling directly above it. In the opposite corner sat a heavy, cluttered desk, and behind the desk sat Major Matthew Hackett, poring over paperwork.

The major was a middle-aged man with short, prematurely iron-gray hair and a thickening waist. He still carried himself well, but there was undeniable dislike in his incisive blue eyes as he glanced up and said, 'What is it now, Kelso?'

Kelso came to a halt before the desk and threw up a salute that was nowhere near as coordinated as he would have liked. 'The man, Crawford. You've heard the news, I suppose?'

'That he took off after his boys in the middle of the night? Of course.'

'I've ordered Lew Eden to go fetch him back.'

'And who gave you the authority to do that?' demanded the major. 'He made his choice, Kelso. He's a civilian. He can pretty much do whatever he likes. It's not up to us to nursemaid him.'

'No, sir. But he's gone after his boys because we weren't able to get them back for him.'

Hackett sighed impatiently. 'We went over all this yesterday. There's nothing we can do if the Apaches skip across the border. Whether we like it or not, our hands are tied. All we can do is accept it.'

'Even if it leaves a bad taste in the mouth, Major?'

'The way you speak, Captain, you sound like you have a *choice* in the matter.'

'Maybe I do, sir. With your blessing. Let me take ten of the best men we've got out on patrol. There's a lot of country out there, Major. We could easily stray across the line and, uh, not realize it.'

'And while you're there, you'd track down Hascha's Apaches and rescue Crawford's boys, is that it?'

'Lew Eden knows approximately where Hascha and his men are holed up. It's possible we could hit them hard and have the boys back here by sunset.'

'It's also possible you and your ten best men will get their backsides blown off, and I'd be left to explain the whole sorry business to Washington,' countered Hackett. 'Forget it, Captain. Conscience is a terrible thing, but I'm not going to risk an international incident just so you can ease yours.'

Anger burned bright in Kelso's eyes, but all he said was, 'What about the strongbox we found by the stagecoach, Major?'

'What about it?'

'The Apaches don't have any use for money, and yet they emptied that box right out.' He paused briefly, then said, 'I reckon that's why they hit the stage in the first place. For the money.'

' . . . which they plan to use to buy weapons, is that it?'

'I can't think of any other reason, Major.'

'It's tempting to try and nip that kind of move in the bud, Captain, I'll grant you that. But the government has had to work long and hard to get the Mexicans to sign a treaty allowing us to resurvey the frontier line west of the Rio Grande. They won't stand for anything that jeopardizes that, it's taken too long.'

'The government doesn't have to know — '

' — not if it all goes as you hope it will, no. But frankly, Kelso, even if I was to go along with it, I really don't think you'd be the best man for the job. Besides, there's been a new development. George Crook has just been reassigned to the Department of Arizona. Washington thinks he's the man to get a handle on our problems with the Apaches, and I agree. In fact, he's due here later today.'

'Here?'

'Why else do you think we're hopping, Kelso? Word came through overnight. He wants to tour the forts and get the lay of the land before he takes up office at Fort Whipple, and he's starting with us.' Hackett's eyes suddenly turned bleak. 'I don't want any trouble while he's here, Captain. Do I make myself clear?'

'Sir,' Kelso said softly.

The major nodded. 'Good. Now, I'm sure you have other duties to perform, as indeed do I. I suggest you go and attend to them.'

'Sir.'

'Oh, and one other thing.'

'Major?'

'If I can smell the rotgut on your breath from here, then it's ten to one the men under your command can smell it as well. If you give me any cause to believe that your intemperance is affecting your duties as an officer, I will have you cashiered so fast it'll make your head spin. Got it?'

Kelso bit back a retort. *Accept it,* he told himself. And squaring his shoulders, he said, 'Yes, sir. Loud and clear.'

*   *   *

Crawford had no idea how long he lay unconscious in the building heat. All he knew was that the silent void into which he had fallen was a far better place than the too-painful here and now, and he was in no hurry to leave it.

Until someone poked him in the ribs.

He tried to ignore it at first, in the hope that whoever it was would believe — as they had believed yesterday — that he was dead, and leave him be.

But then he felt them prodding him more insistently. Someone kicking him in the side.

He felt himself waking up whether he wanted to or not, and as he finally surfaced, opened his bloodshot eyes and focused blearily, he saw that he was surrounded by —

Apaches!

There were three of them, and they were bent forward at the waist with their heads cocked inquisitively, studying him with open puzzlement.

The sight of them brought everything back in a rush and with a cry he lurched up into a sitting position.

To his surprise, the three Apaches leapt away from him, almost fearful, and quickly exchanged alarmed looks. One of them said something in the guttural Apache tongue. The second one, the stocky one with the milk-white left eye, shook his head.

Crawford scrambled to his knees, saw that they had tethered their ponies to some brush a few yards distant, and tied his own stolen mount alongside them.

Desperation now swamping every other consideration, he cried, 'You can help me! You can help me, yes?' And doing his best to mime his meaning, he went on, 'Two boys ... two young boys, white, like me. Yes? They were taken by ... by your people. Taken away? I am their father. Their *fa-ther.* I've come to get them back.'

The Apaches continued to study him with suspicion and fear. But why fear?

Then he had it. Like many Indians, the Apaches were afraid of those they considered crazy — and Crawford guessed that he must look and sound pretty crazy right then, what with his bandaged head and disheveled, parched appearance.

He forced himself to smile at them, so that they'd know he posed no threat. 'My boys,' he said, enunciating every word as deliberately as he could. 'My *sons.* I want them back, yes?'

The third Apache shook his head and waved his left hand, clearly telling him to keep his distance.

Crawford ignored him, took a pace closer, babbling all the while. 'You don't understand. Here, look.' He reached up and tore the bandage from his head. His short dark-blond hair stood up in clumps. He pointed to the puckered gash on his forehead. 'Yesterday . . . you attacked a stagecoach. Stagecoach?'

He mimicked the actions of a coach driver.

'You attacked the coach. I fought back.'

He pretended his right hand was a pistol and mimed firing it, and then imitated a man clutching his chest and staggering.

The Apaches backed off still further. They all wore loose, brightly-colored cotton shirts and drawers, folded headbands and moccasins. One carried an age-worn Spencer carbine. An antiquated .36 caliber Whitney revolver was stuffed behind the waistband of the second. The third was toting a Winchester Model '73.

'There was a fight,' Crawford went on, still matching actions to his words. 'Your people died. Then the coach crashed. One of you climbed up onto the coach and looked inside. I shot him.'

At this the Apaches scowled at each other. The one with the milk-white eye, whose name was Narsimha, studied Crawford closer, recalling the events of the previous day, the way his brother, Hridayesh, had leapt up onto the coach only to have his head blown off.

He looked at the crazy man.

Was he saying that *he* was the one who had killed Hridayesh?

Crawford smiled at him, nodded, once again mimed firing a gun and tumbling backwards. 'I have come to get my sons back, yes?' he said.

But Narsimha was no longer interested in what the white man had to say. He felt that he had heard, and seen, enough.

Gesturing to the *pinda-lik-oyi*, he rattled off something harsh and urgent to his companions. They moved quickly to do his bidding, each grabbing one of Crawford's arms and holding tight.

Crawford immediately panicked and started struggling against them, but it was no good — they were far too strong and he was way too weak.

Narsimha set his Winchester aside, came forward, his lip curling. He let go a stream of Apache that held no meaning for his captive. But the tone said it all. This man, this Apache, was accusing him of something, something he felt strongly about.

When he was through talking he treated Crawford to a spiteful backhander. Crawford's head snapped sideways and he went limp in the arms of his captors, who quickly hoisted him back to his full height.

Crawford looked at the lead Apache again, shook his head, began, 'I don't know what — '

Narsimha hit him again, twice, three times, five, each blow a spiteful crack of knuckles against flesh.

Blood stained Crawford's lips and the tips of his moustache. His face screwed up and his voice became a whine. 'P . . . please . . . I only want my *boys* . . . '

But Narsimha was beyond reason

now. All he could think of was his brother and the manner of his brother's death at the hands of this man; those, and the reaction of Hridayesh's young squaw, Tara, to the news —

He dragged a long, curved, bone-handled knife from its sheath and held the tip close to Crawford's left eye. He said something low and slow, the words grinding out between his clenched, broken teeth. He was making all kinds of promises of pain, Crawford knew; promises he fully intended to keep.

Crawford craned his head back, away from the blade, crying openly now, because if he died then his boys stood no chance at all of ever being rescued.

Narsimha moved the blade over to Crawford's right eye, holding the tip no less than a quarter-inch from the blinking, bloodshot orb. Grinning now, Narsimha carefully set the tip of the blade against the skin between Crawford's eyebrows, let the knife draw a light, gentle line down his nose, down through his moustache, around Crawford's twitching mouth and on to his chin.

Then, without warning, Narsimha's eyes — the seeing one and the blind one — bugged in his head and he yelled right into Crawford's face. It was a bellow of rage, an expression of his overwhelming desire to maim before killing his prisoner.

He grabbed Crawford by the jaw, forced him down to his knees, thrust the prisoner's head back, raised the knife and, chuckling, brought it slowly down toward Crawford's left eye.

' . . . n . . . no . . . no, please . . . I only want my boys . . . that's all I'm asking for . . . '

Lower . . .

Closer . . .

. . . *closer* . . .

A rifle cracked and red meat suddenly punched up out of Narsimha's right shoulder.

The Apache screamed and corkscrewed earthward. At the same moment the

82

tethered horses started tugging at the ties to get away from all the noise, and the two braves holding Crawford released him and snatched at their weapons.

The one on the left grabbed for the Whitney stuffed into his waistband. Another deep blast coughed out across the plain and he flew backward with a shattered breastbone.

The Apache on the right, thinking fast, dropped to his knees, intending to use Crawford as cover until he could retrieve his old carbine. But even as he tried to tuck in behind the dazed man the long gun boomed again and a .44/.40 slug ripped the top right off his head.

The Apache went over backwards with hardly a sigh.

Narsimha, meanwhile, was scrambling across the ground toward his Winchester. He folded his fingers through the lever, dragged the weapon up and around —

A fourth bullet took him in the throat. He gave out a gargling croak of sound and then dropped as if pole-axed.

Crawford felt his eyelids begin to flutter and thought he might pass out again. He fought against the impulse and haphazardly pushed himself up off his knees, where he swayed and absently dashed the tears from his eyes.

Half a minute later a rider appeared from out of the heat-haze to the north, a Winchester carbine braced against his hip, the short barrel pointed skyward. He heeled his white-and-brown pinto gelding to a gallop.

Crawford shielded his eyes from the glare and watched him come closer. He was a bulky man in a brown bib shirt and a tall black hat with a flat brim. He looked to be another Indian, because his face was the color of an old penny.

When he was close enough Lew Eden tightened rein and said, 'You fit enough to ride, Crawford?'

Still faintly bewildered, Crawford nodded. He remembered the man now. He had rode in with that officer, Kelso, the previous evening.

'Then let's go,' said Lew. He threw a quick, searching glance at their surroundings. 'No tellin' how many others're out there, but they'll all come runnin' now they've heard the shots.'

'I — '

'Just fork your damn' horse, Crawford. I'm takin' you back to Whitethorn.'

Mention of the fort made Crawford clench his fists. 'You're not,' he replied with sudden resolve. 'I've got to find my boys.'

'You've *got* to get the hell out of here before any more Apaches show up,' said Lew. 'You sure won't be no good to your boys dead, an' that's how you'll wind up, we don't get the hell out of here right now.'

'I'm not budging,' Crawford said stubbornly. 'I'm going on.'

'Go on, then,' said Lew, turning his horse away. 'But you better make damn' sure you know where you're headed. For the last six miles you been trendin' *away* from where I suspicion they're keepin' your boys.'

The revelation hit Crawford like ice-water and had the desired effect — of making him realize just how futile his well-meaning gesture had been.

'But I've got to get them *back*,' he whispered.

'If we can,' said Lew, 'we will. But we'll do it on better terms than this. Now — you comin' or not?'

Crawford turned away and staggered across to the still-skittish horses. 'I'm coming,' he said.

6

Major Hackett was carrying out a last-minute inspection of the fort when Lew rode in with Crawford sitting his own mount slump-shouldered beside him.

Crawford's body-language told the major everything he needed to know. He saw no need to cross the parade ground and show even cursory interest in Crawford's problems. But before he could go on about his business, Lew angled his pinto toward him and Hackett felt compelled to at least acknowledge their arrival.

'You look like hell, Mr. Crawford.' It was the only thing he could think to say.

Crawford looked down at him through haunted eyes. 'My sons're still going through it,' he replied.

'Yes, I . . . ah . . . I'm sorry about

that. But it's as I tried to explain to you yesterday — '

'Save it,' said Crawford. 'You made your decision. Now you have to live with it.'

He turned his horse away and walked it forlornly toward the infirmary.

Hackett watched him go, his face coloring.

'Major,' said Lew, 'I understand you're expectin' a visitor.'

'I am,' said Hackett, brightening. 'General Crook himself.'

'Then I suggest you look lively,' Lew replied. ''Less I'm much mistaken, his party's on its way in right now. Be here directly.'

Hackett's expression slackened. Here already! And there was still so much to do! George Crook was the closest thing to a legend he was ever likely to encounter, and he wanted everything to be just as perfect as it could be for the General's arrival. God, the man had fought with distinction during the War at such places as Antietam, Hoover's

Gap and Saltville. At the end of hostilities he'd campaigned against the Snake Indians and hit them with a whole new and imaginative set of tactics. The Paiutes, the Pit River Indians, the Modocs, Yavapai and Tonto Apache, the Sioux and Cheyenne . . . he had bested them all, and if any man could subdue the likes of Hascha and Geronimo —

He started across the parade ground at a trot, spotted Kelso and jabbed a finger at him. 'The General's due in any minute,' he said. 'I don't want you anywhere he's likely to see you.'

He moved on, leaving Kelso to watch him go.

The captain stood there for a moment, lacking even the energy it would take to get angry. Somehow, everything had beaten him down. He merely nodded to himself, then headed for the sutler's store. The mighty *Nantan Lupan* was hardly likely to run into him there, he thought — Kelso understood that the man never drank.

The sutler's store was a single-story building constructed from mud-chinked logs and a pitched shingle roof. It was a combination store and saloon, with a plank-and-barrel bar that ran along the right-side wall, a modest scattering of tables and chairs and a line of floor-to-ceiling shelves obscuring the left-side wall, each one packed with everything from tin cups and folded shirts to long johns and canned sardines.

A few men were clustered together at the bar. Conversation died briefly when Kelso stepped inside and ordered a whiskey.

When Lew Eden entered a few minutes later, he found Kelso seated at a corner table, nursing his drink. He sighed, shook his head, then went up to the bar and ordered a small one for himself, mindful that his Seminole blood didn't tolerate alcohol too well. 'Mind if I join you, Cap?' he asked.

Kelso looked up. His eyes had that bleary look Lew and 'most everyone else at Fort Whitethorn had come to know too well. Kelso waved a hand vaguely. 'Help yourself. But be warned — I'm not likely to be much company.'

'I guessed that,' Lew replied mildly. 'Still, sittin' here feelin' sorry for yourself isn't apt to make things any better, Cap.'

'Is that what I'm doing?' asked Kelso. 'Feeling sorry for myself?'

'It's sure what it looks like.'

'Well,' said Kelso, cracking a sour smile, 'I'll drink to that.'

Before he could bring the glass back to his lips, however, he was distracted by the sight of Crook's column filing into the fort.

Beyond the dusty window came a troop of the Sixth Cavalry, riding in columns of two, followed by two limbers, one dragging a two-pounder Hotchkiss gun, the other pulling what appeared to be a tarp-covered Gatling.

A string of mule-drawn supply wagons came next, each one painted pale blue with red wheels.

Bringing up the rear was a battered

ambulance wagon and a single White Mountain Apache astride a small, clean-limbed mustang.

Major Hackett came out of his office to greet the newcomers, spoke to the officer in charge of the escort and then hurried along the line, headed for the ambulance. He gave his tunic one quick tug and brush-down before reaching the back of the wagon, then coming to attention.

As the door swung open Hackett threw up his smartest salute. The man who stepped down from the wagon, who was dressed in a creased, ankle-length canvas duster and a cork helmet, returned it in similar fashion.

So this, Kelso thought, was George Crook.

He studied *Nantan Lupan* over the rim of his whiskey glass. The man was taller than he'd expected, perhaps an even six feet, and he had a lean, sinewy build that made him seem much younger than his four-and-fifty years. He had close-set eyes that mixed gray with blue, a long, aquiline nose and a determined set to his jaw, from which his graying beard parted into two impressive forks.

The woman who followed him down was full-figured, and wore her almost white hair gathered in a bun at the back of her head. She nodded a greeting to Hackett, who took her right hand gently by the fingertips and bowed his head in response. This, Kelso concluded, was doubtless Crook's wife, the former Mary Tapscott Dailey. She had dark brows above kindly brown eyes and a warm yet serene smile.

Crook made the introductions, then indicated the Apache who had been riding behind the ambulance wagon. The Apache was about thirty-five or so, with a dark, flat face framed by greasy, shoulder-length hair that was tied back behind a folded scarlet headband. The headband identified him as a scout, and given his proximity to the General's wagon, Kelso could only suppose that he was Crook's favorite, a man named

Panayatishn, who was more familiarly known as Peaches.

Peaches wore a sober, humorless expression as he surveyed the fort. He was dressed in a cheap white shirt and had his plain cotton pants tucked down inside knee-high moccasins. At his belt he wore an Army .44.

'Want some advice, Cap?' Lew said, drawing him back from what was going on outside.

'Sure,' he slurred. 'Why not?'

'You can't blame Hackett for writing you off as an officer when you act like this.'

Kelso smiled coolly. 'I'm just supposed to . . . *accept* it, am I?'

'That's *exactly* it. Take it, bide your time, wait for the next opportunity to prove yourself.'

'There *are* no opportunities, Mr. Eden.'

'Then *make* them.'

'How am I supposed to do that?'

Lew's mouth tightened. 'We've had this little discussion before, Cap. The

Apaches have the beatin' of us time and again, and for why? Because they travel light and they move fast and we never stand a hope in hell of catching 'em. Now, if we know the answer to the problem, what the hell's keepin' us from doin' somethin' *about* it?'

Kelso shrugged. 'Red tape?'

'Maybe. But that's the thing with tape, Cap. You can cut right through it, if you've a mind.'

'And face a charge of inbusord . . . in-sub-ordi-nation?'

Behind them the door opened and Addison Crawford came inside. Once again the background babble of conversation dropped, then picked up again. Crawford, his head-wound now re-bandaged, looked around the room, let his eyes pass over Kelso and Lew, then went up to the bar and ordered a whiskey.

'You sure that's wise, mister?' asked the sutler, a fat man by the name of Edgar Hill.

'Just give me a god-damned whiskey,'

snapped Crawford, spilling coins on the ring-marked counter.

'All right,' Lew continued, keeping his voice pitched low and confidential. 'So come at it from a different direction. Use a little . . . what do they call it? *Tact*.'

'How's that again?'

'Go see Hackett. Tell him the same thing you and me have discussed more times than I can recall, about how we need to fight the Apache on equal terms. Only this time, you tell him what *he* stands to gain from it. That man has fierce ambition, Cap. Use that to your advantage.'

Kelso cleared his throat wearily. 'It all comes back to opportunity,' he said. 'And Hackett's not likely to give me that.'

A shadow fell across the table. There were no prizes for guessing who it belonged to. Crawford looked down at Lew, then across to Kelso. Then he raised his shot-glass and said, lifting his voice, 'Let me propose a toast.'

Around him, the sutler's store went quiet.

'Crawford . . . ' Lew warned softly.

'To Captain Nathan Kelso,' Crawford continued, ignoring him. 'A man whose word isn't even worth the breath it takes to give it.'

So saying, he flung the contents of the glass in Kelso's face and then threw himself at the man. Kelso went back in his chair, whiskey stinging his eyes, the pain of it sobering him fast, but before Crawford could reach him, Lew sprang up and grabbed him in a restraining bear-hug.

'Whoa, there!' Lew barked, spinning the civilian around. 'Simmer down, Crawford!'

Crawford, however, had no intention of simmering down. He continued to struggle, trying to break Lew's grip so he could go after the man he blamed for all his misfortunes, but Lew wasn't having it.

He looked around, spotted two troopers he knew well and snapped,

'Brady! McGee! Get this man back to the infirmary — and make sure he stays there!'

The men Lew had summoned were complete opposites. One was tall, with a dark spill of hair, a beanpole neck and a prominent Adam's apple. The other was short, skinny, with fair hair and freckles. For a moment they, like everyone else in the store, was transfixed by what had happened, and seeing one of their officers suffer a new low. Then Brady and McGee jumped to it.

'*It's on your conscience!*' screamed Crawford, glaring at Kelso as they dragged him toward the door. '*Whatever becomes of my boys . . . of me . . . you're the one who's got to live with it!*'

The door slammed shut behind them, and once again absolute, awkward silence claimed the store.

All too aware that he had become the center of attention, Kelso sleeved the last of the whiskey off his face. *To Captain Nathan Kelso*, he thought. *A* man *whose word isn't even worth the breath it takes to give it.*

And Hackett, earlier, when he'd tried to get permission to cross the border and rescue the Crawford boys: *Frankly, Kelso, even if I was to go along with it, I really don't think you'd be the best man for the job.*

And just before General Crook arrived: *The General's due in any minute. I don't want you anywhere he's likely to see you.*

Had he really fallen so low?

Lew's voice came back to him. *You can't blame Hackett for writing you off as an officer when you act like this.*

He looked up. His men were watching him. A few were even grinning at his misfortune, while Trooper Carr showed only sympathy.

In a way, that was even worse.

Indeed, for Kelso it was the last straw. He stood up, cursing his own instability, and grabbed his hat.

'Sit back down, Cap,' said Lew. 'I haven't finished with you, yet.'

'Step aside, Lew,' Kelso breathed.

'Give me one good reason.'

Kelso's eyes, still watering from the whiskey, met his. 'Because I'm never going to get a better opportunity than right now to turn this mess around,' he grated softly.

7

When he'd first come to the Arizona Territory, back in the summer of '71, George Crook had been under orders to end hostilities as quickly and peacefully as he could.

He had long held sympathy for his enemies, and felt that they had been treated so poorly by the U.S. Senate that they had been more or less forced to go on the warpath.

The sentiment hardly endeared him to his superiors in Washington, but Crook was nothing if not a soldier, and so he had obeyed his orders and fought, particular the Shoshones and the Nez Percé, even though he would sooner have settled the matter by discussion alone.

He got his chance at discussion during his first major expedition into what had until then been considered enemy territory. Meeting with the likes of Cochise, Pitone and Eskititsla, he had delivered a simple message. Red man and white *had* to learn to live together in peace for the simple reason that more and more whites were settling in lands traditionally ruled by the Indians, and the Indians, he said, couldn't hope to stop the westward expansion, any more than they could win against such overwhelming numbers.

Besides, most of the whites were good people, just as were most Indians. But there were bad apples in every barrel, and he would do his best to deal with the bad whites if the chiefs would do as much for him in return.

The Indians had respected his directness, and a peace of sorts was brokered. But there was fighting, too, and during that fighting the hold-outs saw the tough, determined side of George Crook.

Within four years it was over, and Crook received new orders; to go north and take command of the Department of the Platte, there to lock horns with the Sioux and Cheyenne.

Now the general said, 'It is, of course, important to remember that the Apaches are but one facet of this business, Major.'

Hackett, sitting across the desk from him, listened with rapt attention. Mary Crook had been shown to temporary lodgings in the married quarters and then Crook himself had announced his desire to discuss the present situation with the Apaches. Now they were sitting in Hackett's office and doing exactly that.

'To the general populace,' the general went on, 'they are savages, drunk on blood and violence. Certainly they are cruel, by our standards. But they are also a good, proud people, Major. They fight because they see no other course open to them. They feel cornered, betrayed, overwhelmed . . . and with good reason.' He frowned suddenly. 'You have heard of the Tucson Ring, of course?'

Hackett nodded. 'Yes, General. A

group of influential merchants who are said to keep hostilities going by any means possible because it's good for trade. But I'm not entirely sure they really exist.'

'Oh, they exist, all right, Major, and they've been at their chicanery for years. But because they are so powerful, and have the ears of some very prominent politicians, the authorities have turned a blind eye to them. They profit from just about every aspect of this conflict, Major. They sell arms and ammunition to us *and* the Indians. They sell cattle that should rightly be sent to the reservations to the more lucrative markets in the north. They cheat the government *and* the Indians every way they can, because if this war stops, their gravy train stops right along with it.' He smiled grimly. 'They've been busy in my absence, and now I have to reestablish the peace I left behind me seven years ago.'

Silence settled between them.

'Well, so much for the background,'

the general continued. 'The reason I am here now, Major, is because I always like to speak personally with the officers under my command, get to know the situation as they see it, the ideas they have for dealing with it, the kind of men at their disposal and the state of their morale.'

'Certainly, General. I have to say — '

He broke off as the sound of raised voices reached them from outside. Hackett heard Lieutenant Miller saying, 'No, you can't — '

But that was as far as his adjutant got. A second later the door opened and — Hackett experienced a flash of pure fury — Nathan Kelso came inside . . . bringing the stench of whiskey with him.

The major sprang out of his chair, demanded, 'Kelso! What is the meaning of this?'

Ignoring the question, Kelso stood to attention and snapped a salute in Crook's direction, holding it there until the faintly bemused general finally returned it.

'Permission to address the general, sir?' he asked.

Hackett came angrily around the desk. 'No, you may *not* have permission to address the general, sir! You can apologize for your unseemly conduct and then turn tail and get out of here!'

But Kelso stood his ground, addressing Crook directly. 'General, may I have a word? It won't take long.'

Crook studied him. Kelso looked like a wreck, a disgrace to his uniform and a man who stank to high heaven of liquor. And yet when he looked into the young captain's eyes he saw fire there — not anger, but passion — and he was intrigued.

'Very well, Captain,' he said softly.

Hackett immediately turned to him. 'I can only apologize for this man, General. *Lieutenant!* Remove Captain Kelso immediately!'

'Just a moment, Hackett,' said Crook mildly. 'I'll hear this man out first.'

'Thank you, General,' said Kelso.

At a nod from Hackett, Lieutenant

Miller closed the door and left them alone.

'All right,' said Crook. 'I'll give you one minute exactly.'

To underline the condition, Hackett took out his gold half-hunter and checked the second-hand.

'Yesterday a band of Apaches led by a renegade named Hascha hit the noon stage to Fortuna,' said Kelso.

'Hascha,' muttered Crook. 'He wields influence with Geronimo, so I believe.'

'Yes, sir. The Indians killed the crew and three of the four passengers, and emptied out the strongbox. That was the main purpose of the raid in my opinion, sir — to obtain money with which to buy weapons.'

'The Tucson Ring again,' Crook muttered to Hackett. 'Go on.'

'The Apaches also took two prisoners, sir, boys, one aged seven, the other nine. My patrol gave chase, but unfortunately they had the beating of us and crossed the border into Sonora.'

'There's nothing we can do about that.'

'No, sir. But we might be able to keep it from ever happening again.'

'Oh? How so, captain?'

'The Apaches are tough and resourceful, sir. They're flexible and extraordinarily mobile, because *they* travel light, and *we* don't.'

'You have fifteen seconds left,' said Hackett, with no small relish.

'When you first came to the Territory, sir, you introduced the concept of mules to the army because they are tough and hardy and can move over terrain a horse would normally find difficult. You introduced Apache scouts to — '

'Time's up,' Hackett announced. 'Now get out of here, Kelso. I'll deal with you later.'

'Wait,' said Crook. 'Go on, captain.'

Kelso took a breath. 'You introduced Apache scouts in the correct belief that it would *take* an Apache to *find* an Apache, and it worked. Well, in the same way, sir, I believe that by creating a unit within our own ranks that is capable of travelling light and moving fast, a unit as flexible as the very Apaches we're after, we can turn the tide of this war, sir. And I for one am all for that.'

'And how would you propose to create such a unit?'

'At the moment we carry supplies when we could just as easily live off the land. We carry oats for our mounts when they could just as easily forage, in the short term. We carry tents when we could just as easily sleep under the stars. If we cut our equipment down to the bare minimum, sir, we become lighter, faster, more able to fight the Indians on an equal footing.'

Crook made no immediate response. He dropped his chin to his chest and thought for a long moment. Then he said, 'Major . . . would you step outside for a moment? I'd like to speak with Captain . . . Kelso, is it? Captain Kelso, alone.'

Hackett didn't like it, but knew better

than to let it show. 'I'll be right outside,' he said, and let Kelso have his fiercest glare before he quit the room.

When they were alone, Crook said, 'You're quite the firebrand, aren't you, Kelso.'

'No sir.'

'Then what are you? Aside from a drunk?'

Kelso let that pass. 'I'm a soldier, sir. A soldier who, just like every other soldier on this post and, I suspect, right across this Territory, is sick and tired of letting the Apaches hold the upper hand.'

'But there's more to it than that, isn't there?' said Crook, perceptively. 'Is it these boys you mentioned?'

'They're part of it, sir. A fair part of it.'

'You know you can't cross that line and get them back.'

'Yes, sir.'

'So what else is it, then? The other part?'

Kelso felt his posture soften a little,

and kept his eyes forward. 'I would sooner not say, sir.'

'Revenge?' hazarded Crook. 'Is that it? You want to get back at the Apaches for taking the boys?'

'No, sir. If you must know . . . '

'Go on,' said Crook. 'I'm listening.'

'You are a religious man, sir.'

'I am, indeed.'

'I am not, sir. But I believe I understand the value of . . . ' He could hardly bring himself to say it, but it was the truth and as such it couldn't be denied. ' . . . of *salvation*, sir,' he said quietly.

Crook considered that, his expression giving nothing away. Then: 'You're a mess, Captain, and frankly I'd be a fool to grant you permission to go ahead and do *anything* other than sober up.'

Kelso nodded, thought, *Accept it*, and said only, 'Very good, General. Thank you, sir.'

'I haven't finished yet,' said Crook. 'You're a mess. But that's not to say you can't change. How many men do you need?'

Kelso could hardly believe his ears. 'Thirty, sir,' he replied quickly. 'The best horsemen we have on the post — volunteers, preferably.'

'Will Major Hackett spare you thirty men, if you can get them?'

'I doubt it, sir.'

'Then we'll split the difference. If you can get fifteen men to ride with you, you've got your chance. But I'll be honest with you, Captain — given the state of you, I'll be surprised if you can find that many men who're willing to take your orders. And even if you do, you've still got to prove yourselves to my satisfaction before I'll recognize your unit. Do I make myself clear?'

'Yes, sir.'

'Very good. Now get out of here, clean yourself up — and go recruit your men.'

'Sir.'

Kelso turned and left the room.

Crook watched the door for a long

moment after he'd gone, the expression on his lean face almost troubled. Then Major Hackett came back in, full of apologies.

'I am so sorry, General. I will see to it that Captain Kelso is — '

' — given everything he requires,' Crook finished.

Hackett's mouth opened and closed like that of a landed carp. 'Beg pardon, General?'

'I think that young man may be just what we need to turn this war around,' said Crook. 'But not necessarily in the way he believes.'

8

Addison Crawford didn't wake early. To do that you had to fall asleep first, and sleep had eluded him ever since the attack on the stage.

He hadn't believed the hours of darkness could pass so slowly. He'd stared up at the infirmary's dark ceiling and thought about Joseph and Ira. It was a torment, wondering where they were and what they were feeling right now, and whether or not the influence of their new surroundings was already beginning to change them from the boys he had always known and loved.

From outside came the strains of *Reveille,* followed shortly thereafter by the sounds of the fort coming to life. Crawford sat up and sighed. *Reveille, Retreat, Supper Call, Taps.* Just as Joseph and Ira were already adjusting to life among the Apaches, he was adjusting to life here at Whitethorn.

At last, feeling helpless and frustrated, he got up and wandered to the window that was even now starting to fill with the watery light of false dawn.

His attention was taken almost immediately by the sight of Sergeant Shannon leading a knot of eighteen shuffling soldiers across the parade ground toward the sutler's store. Among them were the two soldiers who'd dragged him from the sutler's store the previous afternoon.

Just then a rider entered the fort from the direction of town. Crawford's mouth thinned as he identified Lew Eden. He knew his dislike of the man was irrational. Eden had saved his life yesterday, no doubt about it. But right now Crawford didn't think his life was worth living if it meant living it without his sons.

Out on the parade ground Shannon saw Lew coming and stopped a while to watch as he walked his horse closer.

'What's goin' on, Sarge?' the half-breed asked as he dismounted.

Shannon shook his head. 'Beats me. The captain spent yesterday afternoon in the adjutant's office, goin' through the records. Then he gave me a list with your name right alongside these other fellers and told me to get you all to the sutler's store at dawn.'

Lew stared at the building thoughtfully, then said, 'Well, let's go see what's on his mind.'

'Perhaps he wants to buy us all a drink,' someone hazarded from among the knot of enlisted men.

'Stow that kind of talk!' barked Shannon.

Kelso was waiting for them as they filed in, some yawning, others still rubbing at their sleep-puffed eyes, and found themselves chairs. The store was empty this early in the day, Edgar Hill rummaging busily in his adjoining stockroom.

Kelso looked at the men whose records he had pored over the day

116

before. They threw him curious looks in return, wondering why he'd summoned them. He decided not to keep them in suspense.

'You're here because you're the best horsemen we've got at Whitethorn,' he said, 'and because you've got pluck. If you decide to accept my offer — and it *is* an offer, I'm only taking volunteers — you'll need both.'

The men exchanged puzzled or apprehensive looks.

'I'm sick of letting the Apaches run rings around us,' he went on, 'and I think you men feel the same way. But now we've been given a chance to do something about it, to fight them on their own terms, as a special unit that'll travel light and hit the enemy hard wherever it finds them. If we can get results, it'll become permanent. Who's with me?'

This, Kelso knew, was the moment of truth. It was as Crook had said — it all depended on whether or not he could get fifteen men to follow him. But who wanted to follow a borderline drunk?

There was no immediate response to his offer, and he felt his spirits drop, though he could hardly say he was especially surprised. Then Trooper Reuben Brady, the lanky, dark-haired former cowboy from Texas, raised his hand.

'Go ahead, Brady.'

'Do we get paid extra for riskin' our skins, Cap'n?'

'No. Maybe later, once we've proven our worth. But not right now.'

'Captain?'

The speaker was Trooper Carr. Carr had been a veterinarian until his twin brother was killed by Ute Indians back in '79, alongside Indian agent Nathan Meeker and nine other men at the White River Agency in Colorado. In what became known as the Meeker Massacre, the Utes had also taken prisoners, three women and two children.

'If I sign up, do we go after those two boys?' he asked in his usual soft, polite manner. 'Crawford's kids?'

Kelso shook his head. 'Nothing would give me greater pleasure, Trooper, but no. We can't. Major Hackett and General Crook have already made that plain.'

'Too bad,' said Carr.

Another hand raised. Kelso identified Trooper Porter Fitch, a short, barrel-chested one-time blacksmith who wasn't really built for riding but was nonetheless good in the saddle and knew horses well. 'It occurs to me,' said Fitch, 'that if things get as rough and ready as you think they will, then we'd have to rely on each other even more than we do already.'

'That's right.'

'Well, don't think I'm speakin' out of turn . . .'

'Go on.'

'Can we rely on *you*, Cap'n?'

You could see he hated to be the one to say it, but he was only voicing what was in all their minds

'I mean, what with you leadin' us, an' all.'

Kelso drew a breath. He'd asked

himself the same question, more than once, since his meeting with Crook, and though he wanted to tell them that of course they could rely on him, he was by no means sure. He hadn't touched a drink since yesterday . . . but that didn't mean to say he hadn't wanted to.

'Me, I say we give the man a chance.'

The speaker was Veniamin Baranski, whom his comrades called Benny. He shoved forward, a giant of a man, his beard thick and black as midnight. In his native Ukraine he had been a Cossack — the warriors who made up the cavalry of the czars.

Baranski continued in his deep, ponderous way, 'I don' think the *Kapeetan* he let us down. He good man, in here.' He tapped his chest. 'Besides . . . if one of us die' because of his bad leadership, the rest would see that the *Kapeetan,* he die' as well, *da?*'

Kelso bit back a response. He needed these men, almost at any cost, and they were right. He could hardly offer them his word not to let them down. That had become a useless currency. So he said, 'It's a deal, Baranski. If I foul up, if I let you men down in any way, then I pay the price. But remember this, all of you; the trail runs both ways. You men do like I say, when I say, and we'll give the Indians a run for their money. But you'll all pull your weight.'

Silence fell again as the men digested that. Swallowing, Kelso said, 'I'll leave you to think about it, talk it over. When you've made up your minds, come find me and let me know what you've decided.'

'I'll let you know right now, Cap,' said Lew Eden, speaking for the first time from where he was leaning against the bar. 'If you're givin' me the chance to give a sumbitch like Hascha a taste of his own medicine, I'm with you all the way.'

'Thanks, Lew.'

As he crossed to the door, Trooper Cyrus McGee stopped him. 'You, ah, got a name for this unit, Cap'n?' he asked. He had been a jockey once, back east, and from all accounts a very successful one.

Kelso looked at him, the word *no* on his lips. Then he stopped and allowed himself a brief smile. 'Yeah,' he replied instead. 'We're named after General Crook, the man who gave us this chance in the first place. We're going to be known as Company C.'

★   ★   ★

Kelso left them to discuss it, hoping they'd throw in with him and knowing they probably wouldn't. He wanted a drink but not so badly that he couldn't control the need. As he headed for the officers' mess he spotted General Crook's Apache, Peaches, watching him from the shade of a stable doorway and nodded acknowledgement. Peaches appeared to look straight through him.

As he continued on, he noticed Crawford standing just outside the infirmary. Even from this distance he could feel hostility radiating off the man.

For a moment he considered going over there and trying to make his peace with the printer. But what could he really say? He had no words to adequately describe what it had meant to him not to be able to keep his word, and doubted that Crawford would let him speak anyway.

He went into the mess, poured himself some coffee, then sat alone at one of the long bench tables and tried not to think what would become of him if the men he'd hand-picked for this job rejected him. Without the support and respect of his men, an officer was nothing — and Kelso realized suddenly that he had been nothing to these men for far too long, and hated the knowledge.

About ten minutes later a sound woke him from his reverie. He looked out through one of the dusty windows, saw Lew Eden and the other men leaving the sutler's store. They'd reached their decision, then.

Kelso watched them cross the parade-ground with Lew and Shannon at their head. Lew was already with him, he knew. But the rest . . . ?

He stood up, went to the doorway on legs that felt more like wooden blocks to find out what was going to happen.

The men gathered around Lew and Shannon, thirteen of them. The other five were nowhere to be seen.

'Cap,' said Lew. 'Few of the boys didn't care too much for your plan. But me an' the rest of these fellers . . . we kinda like the sound of Company C.'

Thirteen . . .

Kelso cursed his luck. Crook had told him he could go ahead if he could get fifteen men to follow him. He was two short . . . and that meant that he'd failed.

Again.

But then he took another look at them. Thirteen men . . . plus Lew . . . plus Shannon . . .

Fifteen!

Suddenly it was all he could do not

to sag. As it was, he let his pent-up breath go in a low, relieved sigh, although he was careful to keep that relief off his face. They didn't need to know just how desperate he really was.

'All right, you men,' he said. 'Thank you. But you may regret your decision before this is over. You're all fine horsemen. That was one of the reasons I picked you in the first place. But beginning from today, you're going to get even better. And when you can ride as well if not better than a Cheyenne Dog Soldier, you'll be ready. So go get yourselves some breakfast . . . and then we'll get started.'

* * *

Kelso began as he meant to go on. He had the men assemble in one of the corrals behind the stable and led out a horse that was fully outfitted and ready to ride.

'Only trouble is,' he said, 'it's too top-heavy to stand any chance of keeping up with the Apaches, and nowhere near as maneuverable. So we've got to shed some weight here.'

He began by ditching the half-tent and pole that every man was required to carry, tearing them off the saddle and tossing them to the ground at his feet. 'It won't hurt us to sleep outdoors,' he said. 'And if the weather turns bad, we'll find cover or we'll get wet.'

Next came the greatcoat and spare clothes, the brush and shoe pouch, the forage sack filled with grain or sometimes corn. 'There's enough forage out there for the horses,' he said, jerking his chin in the general direction of the desert. 'And no one in their right mind expects us to shine our shoes while we're on patrol.'

As the men continued to watch, he discarded the picket-pin and lariat, the provision-filled haversack. 'No call to weigh ourselves down with hardtack, coffee and bacon. We can just as easily live off the land in the short term.' He also said that they would do away with the kettles, skillets and coffee-pots some of the men were apt to carry when out in the field, and share a single set of implements.

What remained of their gear, he went on, should be distributed more evenly, since the present arrangement tended to put more weight on the saddle's near side, which became even more of a liability because that was the side the men were apt to pull toward them when mounting.

Porter Fitch, the burly blacksmith, now warmed to the subject. He suggested they do away with the McClellan's quarter-straps, spider rings and cinches. 'You fit a single girth to leather billets,' he said, 'you automatically make it lighter.'

Kelso considered that and saw another benefit besides. 'It'll make it quicker to saddle up, too.'

The other men, caught up in the moment, began to pitch in. Reuben Brady was of the opinion that the hooded stirrup leathers were too heavy and the buckles too large. The hood itself served no practical purpose and if it were removed, that would reduce the weight still further.

Cyrus McGee said that they could also get by with smaller saddle blankets. The present issue blanket took six folds before it could sit comfortably beneath the saddle. A smaller one would weigh less and be easier to use.

While their saddles were sent to the tack shop, where Fitch was ordered to oversee the changes, the rest of the men were put to work building a crude obstacle course which Kelso had spent the previous evening designing. By the time it was finished it was a curious-looking affair, but it would test horse and rider both and force them to master changing gaits and sudden turns.

In all it was a long, demanding day. Their horses were used to noise and activity, but Kelso had the men fire off guns within their vicinity and run around them whooping and hollering to get them even more used to it. At Trooper Carr's suggestion, the horses received praise afterwards and were given chopped apples and carrots as rewards.

Pleased with the way things were shaping up so far, Kelso finally told the men to go grab something to eat and then have one drink on him at the sutler's store.

'You joinin' us, Cap'n?' asked Trooper Quillan. He made it sound more like a challenge.

'I'll pass,' Kelso replied.

As the men walked off, Lew hung back and said, 'Well, what do you reckon?'

'I reckon we could really make something of this,' said Kelso. 'But I could sure do without the audience.'

'Crawford,' said Lew, without looking around.

Kelso nodded. 'He's been standing over there on the far side of the corral for the past hour, just watching us,' he said. 'Likely wondering why we're wasting our time on all this crazy stuff when we should be out after his boys.'

When they finally turned and looked at Crawford, the printer simply limped away.

But Kelso had guessed the nature of Crawford's thoughts correctly. Crawford just couldn't understand how someone like Kelso, a drunk if all the fort gossip was to be believed, a man who had given his word and broken it, could be rewarded with a new command. It just didn't make sense. The army was supposed to be there to protect the populace, but it had done nothing to protect Crawford or his boys.

He had realized that, in the face of the army's seeming indifference to his plight, he was going to have to rescue his boys alone. His first attempt had been a shambles, of course. He hadn't been thinking straight, had allowed his emotions to cloud his normally good judgment.

Next time it would be different. He had money in the Ocotillo Creek bank, enough to buy a good horse, a couple of mules, an assortment of cheap gewgaws and other such items with which he would try to buy back his sons. If the gewgaws didn't work, then he would offer the Apaches something they could not resist — guns. And if that's what it took to get his boys back, he'd buy them a whole damn' arsenal of them.

But he was going to have to be careful this time, and not make the mistakes he'd made before.

He left Whitethorn behind him and headed back into town. His thoughts were dark and vengeful.

* * *

Early next morning the men of Company C saddled up, inspected their newly-modified hulls and offered their approval, even Baranski. 'Is good, *Kapeetan*,' he rumbled. 'We ride like Cossacks now, *da?*'

'I don't know,' Kelso replied. 'Why don't you show us how a Cossack rides, Benny?'

Baranski studied the obstacle course before them. On first inspection it looked like a jumble of laid-flat wagon wheels, hay-bales upon which planks of wood had been balanced at different heights, a canvas wagon-shroud spread loosely across the ground and weighted down at its corners by rocks, with a few crude scarecrow-figures with pumpkin heads planted here and there, some scattered buckets that seemed to serve no real purpose and four breeze-blown sandbags swaying back and forth from the lowest branch of a nearby sun-bleached oak. But when you looked closer you could see a definite course marked between all the obstacles.

Baranski's dark eyes lit with pleasure and a wide grin split his curly black beard. 'Sure,' he said, checking the tightness of his horse's girth-strap one last time. '*Pochemu by i net?*'

As soon as the last word left his

mouth he sprang onto his horse's back and the animal leapt into a gallop.

While the other men cheered him on, Baranski's horse wheeled right, around the first wagon-wheel, Baranski leaning to the right with it. Then the animal surged on toward the first of the plank-and-hay-bale jumps. The horse took it easily, came down, galloped on, took the second, higher jump, landed a little unsteadily.

When Baranski guided the horse left around the second wheel, the animal slewed noticeably and Baranski was quick to shift his weight to that side. But as the animal approached the flattened wagon-shroud a stray gust of wind sent an unexpected ripple through the material and instinctively the horse shied, slowed, sidestepped and, in so doing, kicked one of the buckets over. The clatter the bucket made only unnerved the animal further, and suddenly Baranski had all he could do just to get it to calm down again.

This drew a few good-natured

cat-calls, which Baranski dismissed with an angry swipe of one massive hand. Then he walked the horse back to the others. 'I try again, *da?*' he said. 'This time I do better.'

'Let's see the cap'n do it!' called Trooper Quillan.

Amazingly Kelso sensed no animosity in the challenge, and took it willingly. At no time had he ever expected his men to do anything he wouldn't, or couldn't, do himself. So he reached out and took the reins from Baranski, then toed in to the modified stirrup and mounted up.

Silence settled over the men as they watched him tighten rein and turn the horse back toward the obstacle course. Then —

'*Yaaahh!*'

The horse took off like a bullet from a gun, swept right, around the first wagon-wheel, blurred on toward the first of the plank-and-hay-bale jumps.

Kelso pulled back on the reins and the horse took the obstacle with room to spare and made it look easy. The animal came down, ran on, launched itself at the second, higher jump, cleared it — just — and then followed the curve of the second wheel toward the weighted-down wagon-shroud.

This time it ran straight across the rippling canvas, on toward the third tight turn. The turn took horse and rider directly beneath the swaying sandbags, which Kelso somehow managed to dodge, and then, clumsily, he tore his saber from its scabbard, surged on, threw a reckless swing at one of the scarecrow pumpkin heads.

He missed the target, dismissed it with a frustrated curse and tried to focus on the next obstacle. But there was no time for that. All at once the horse was launching itself gamely at the third jump, but its forelegs hit the plank and knocked it down with a clatter. The horse itself stumbled and slowed, its momentum gone.

Grudgingly the men clapped as Kelso walked his mount back toward them.

'Well, I think that proves the point,' he said as he swung down. 'We're by no means bad . . . but we can, and will, do better.'

Sergeant Shannon bawled, '*Next man!*' and McGee, the one-time jockey, came forward, eager to show his worth.

He turned out to be the best rider of the bunch, but the obstacle course proved difficult even for him.

Still, the men were nothing if not game, and Kelso watched as Shannon sent them all back time and again — even Lew — to master the turns and judge when the time was right to trade a gallop for a canter, a canter for a trot, a trot for a walk.

The day passed in a cloud of dust. Sweat glistened on flushed faces and darkened blue shirts at armpits and back. No horses were injured, but the men's pride took more than a few knocks. Kelso was no exception, and he pushed himself as hard if not harder than anyone else to improve his proficiency in the saddle.

As the afternoon wore on there was a definite improvement in everyone, and when the strains of *Supper Call* drifted across the fort, the mood was buoyant.

As Kelso dismissed the men, Lieutenant Miller came across from the admin block, studying the course dubiously.

'Help you, Lieutenant?' asked Kelso.

Miller nodded. 'General Crook wants to see you in Major Hackett's office right away.'

Something in Miller's tone stirred unease in Kelso. The general probably wanted nothing more than a progress report. But what if he'd had a change of heart, and decided not to continue with Company C after all? Even as the notion occurred to him, he could see his own concerns mirrored in the faces of Lew and Sergeant Shannon.

With more than a few misgivings Kelso followed the lieutenant back across the parade, hastily slapping dust from his shirt and pants. He wanted to ask the lieutenant if he knew why Crook had summoned him, but knew that Miller would claim ignorance if only to prolong his agony.

At last Miller led him across the ante-room, rapped on the door to Major Hackett's adjoining office and opened it when Crook called, 'Come.'

Kelso went past the lieutenant, presented himself before the major's desk, behind which Crook was poring over a pile of dispatches, and threw up a salute that was considerably neater than his previous attempt.

'I apologize for my appearance, General, but my men and I have been working hard today.'

'So I believe,' said Crook, returning the salute. 'Take the weight off, Captain. I've got something I want to discuss with you.'

'About Company C, sir?'

Crook smiled briefly. 'Named after me, so I hear.'

'I thought it was only fitting, sir. The men wanted to know what their new unit was called and . . . well, it just sounded right.'

Crook nodded. 'Quite.'

He fell silent and once again Kelso felt a stirring of apprehension. When Crook still said nothing, he asked respectfully, 'What was it you wanted to discuss with me, sir?'

Crook's next words were the last he'd been expecting to hear.

'Your first assignment,' he said. 'At dawn tomorrow I'm sending you and your men out into the field, Kelso.'

9

Kelso's immediate reaction was to tell Crook that it was too soon, that they'd only just started training and hadn't even touched on tactics yet, but instead he said nothing, because he knew he might never get a chance like this again.

'What are your orders, sir?' he said after a moment.

Crook sat back. 'Have you met my wife, Mary?'

'I've not had that pleasure, sir, no.'

'Well, you're *going* to,' Crook replied. 'As you are aware, she has accompanied me here from Omaha, and Major Hackett has put adequate quarters at our disposal, but since I have decided to stay on at Whitethorn for a while longer, I feel that Mary would be more comfortable in Lukeville.'

Kelso frowned.

'We have friends there,' explained Crook.

'So you want Company C to act as an escort?' said Kelso. 'To make sure she gets there safely?'

'*If* you think your men are up to the task.'

'Well, of course they are, sir.'

But, he wanted to add, *we're supposed to be soldiers, not nurse-maids.*

'Then those, Captain, are your orders,' Crook continued briskly. 'Make sure Mrs. Crook reaches Lukeville safely.' He leaned forward again. 'And don't look so despondent, Kelso. Do you think I'd entrust my wife to any old unit?'

Kelso relaxed a little. 'No, sir. And I thank you for your faith in us. But . . . '

'Go on.'

'Well, Lukeville's about a hundred and seventy miles southeast of here. To reach it we have to follow the border pretty much every step of the way.'

'Do you have a problem with that?'

'Only that I have thirteen men, one sergeant and a scout at my disposal. If the Apaches should cross the border at any time during our journey — '

' — you will let them know they've been in a fight,' Crook finished.

'That we will, sir.'

'Then it's settled.'

Still trying to hide his surprise, Kelso said, 'Very good, General.'

Lew and Shannon were waiting for him when he stepped back out into the sunset. 'You can stop fretting now,' he said as they started back toward the stables together. 'We've just been given our first mission.'

'Judas, that was quick!' murmured Shannon.

'Well, don't get too excited, Sergeant. The general's wife's going on to Lukeville, and we're riding shotgun on her.'

Lew scowled. 'Just Company C?'

'Just Company C.'

'That man must have a lot of faith in us.'

'Thanks.'

'I mean, that's Indian country, Cap. With a *vengeance*.'

'Then we'll just have to be extra vigilant,' said Kelso. Dusk had fallen, and the stars were already starting to show faintly beyond the cerulean sky. 'We leave at first light tomorrow,' he went on. 'So I'm going to spend tonight studying the maps, deciding the best route and making sure we know the locations of all the waterholes along the way. Let the men know what's going on, Sergeant, and tell them to expect to be out in the field for two weeks.'

'How will the lady be travelin', Cap'n?'

'The same way she arrived, I guess. In that ambulance.' He broke stride. 'That's a point. Better have it checked over, and make sure we're packing enough supplies so that she doesn't have to go without. As for the rest of us — '

'I think we got the message by now,'

Lew muttered dryly. 'The rest of us travel *light*.'

'Except for ammunition,' Shannon said grimly. 'Could be we might need that, afore this is over.'

Kelso nodded. 'Agreed.'

He left his companions and headed for his quarters. It had been a long day and there was still a lot left to do. General Crook had indeed put a lot of faith in him, in *all* of them. Maybe Peaches, whom he'd often spotted watching them over the past two days, had reported favorably on their progress.

He suddenly felt some of the darkness lifting from his mood. What surprised him even more was that not once throughout the day had he felt the need for a drink. He wanted to believe that he'd turned a corner at long last, but didn't hold out too much hope.

He was just about to let himself into his quarters when a gun blasted somewhere in the darkness behind him, and something smashed him in the side of the head.

For one small part of a second there was nothing at all, no pain, no feeling. Then —

The agony exploded white hot and all-consuming. He groaned, fell against the door, slid down it, the side of his face burning with a scorching spill of blood —

Dimly he was aware that the gun-blast had brought the fort to life. Men were yelling, others were running back and forth. Someone grabbed him by the shoulders and asked him a question he couldn't immediately grasp.

'Cap'n! Cap'n!'

It was Shannon.

'All . . . right . . . ' Kelso managed. 'I'm . . . all right . . . '

'Here,' said Shannon, gruffly, 'let me be the judge o' that.'

He turned Kelso around none-too-gently, tilted his aching head and inspected it. 'Sonofabitch!' he muttered.

'Wh . . . what is it?'

'You're leakin' like a stuck pig,' reported Shannon.

He dragged out a kerchief and pressed it hard against the left side of Kelso's head in order to staunch the flow.

There was more uproar coming from behind the mess hall, another shot, more yelling.

'Is it . . . bad?' Kelso asked.

'One inch to the left and the bullet would've missed you completely,' said the sergeant. 'One inch to the right and it would've blowed your brains right out. As it is, it's taken the lobe off your ear.'

Kelso wanted to feel relief, but was still hurting too bad. 'Wh . . . who shot me?' he asked.

The sound of raised voices was nearer now. Shannon turned his head so that he could see out across the parade ground, where Lew Eden, followed by a crowd of angry or just plain curious enlisted men, was shoving

146

a cowed civilian ahead of him.

'Can't you guess?' Shannon asked, and spat.

Kelso's heart was racing. 'Not Crawford?'

'Yup — Crawford.' Shannon spat into the dirt. ''Pears that sonofabitch jus' tried to kill you, Cap'n.'

★   ★   ★

The moon-faced sergeant got Kelso to his feet and helped him across to the infirmary, where the post surgeon, Dr. Sutton, stripped off his blood-soaked shirt and then went to work patching him up. Major Hackett stamped in shortly thereafter and demanded to know what in blue blazes was going on.

'Addison Crawford tried to kill the cap'n,' said Shannon. Kelso was in no position to answer the question himself; it was all he could do not to yell as Sutton cleaned the wound thoroughly with carbolic and then set about suturing the ragged flesh to close it against infection.

'I gathered *that* much,' Hackett replied witheringly. 'Eden's had the man thrown into the guardhouse. What I want to know is *why* he tried to kill you.'

The answer to that was so obvious that Kelso was amazed the other man hadn't worked it out for himself. 'He blames me for not getting his boys back,' he managed at last.

'Well, I intend to see that he's charged with attempted murder.'

'I won't press that charge, major.'

'*What?*'

'I won't press charges,' Kelso repeated. How could he, given the circumstances? 'But I've got nothing against you keeping him locked up for a while. Right now that man's a danger to himself as much as anyone else.'

Lew came in just as the surgeon snipped the catgut. He said, 'You never spoke a truer word, Cap. I jus' been questionin' Crawford. Seems that right after he settled *your* hash, he was fixin' to light out, cross the border and try to buy his sons back. He's got a horse an' two pack-mules tethered back in that bosk just east of here.'

'An' what was he hoping to use for currency?' demanded Hackett. 'A few trinkets?'

'Guns,' said Lew. 'If all them trinkets didn't work. He was gonna try to buy his boys back with a batch of Winchesters.'

'The man's insane,' breathed Hackett.

'With grief, maybe.'

'Well, at the very least I'll see that he's charged with treason.'

'Don't mean to speak out of turn, Major,' said Lew, 'but some folks might think that's akin to kickin' a man while he's down.'

Dr. Sutton finally stepped back to study his handiwork. 'I have some good news for you, Captain. I do believe you're going to survive. Of course, your ear will be about as sore as a mashed thumb for the next week or so.'

'Thanks, doc.'

'Go rest up now. You lost quite a bit of blood.'

'I will,' said Kelso, intending to do no such thing.

A new concern suddenly entered Hackett's thinking. 'Will you be fit to ride tomorrow, Captain?'

Kelso nodded. 'Take more than this to slow me down,' he replied, trying to sound more confident than he felt.

★   ★   ★

Kelso went slowly back to his quarters and by lamplight plotted the course they'd have to take to reach Lukeville until he could no longer keep his eyes open. Somewhere along the way he dozed off over his small desk and woke up with the map stuck to the side of his face a little after four the next morning. He turned down the lamp, got up and went over to the chamber set, where he washed and shaved in ice-cold water.

Inspecting himself in the mirror, he

saw that the wound to his ear had dried to a crust the color of fine burgundy. It was sore to the touch and ached like hell. He also felt a little unsteady because of the amount of blood he'd lost, but figured that would pass as he made it back up.

He breakfasted lightly in the officer's mess, still preoccupied by the mission ahead of him. By the time he'd finished, the ambulance which was to transport the general's wife had been brought around to the front of the married quarters by her driver, a thin, elderly trooper named Corbett, who had bushy white brows and a steer-horn moustache of the same color.

Inside the stable Kelso found the men of Company C preparing their mounts for travel. They seemed in high spirits, perhaps because there would be no more drill until their journey to Lukeville was over. He answered all their enquiries about his health and then saddled his own sleek, fifteen-hand bay horse.

By the time he and the men led their mounts across to the ambulance, Mary Crook was bidding a tearful goodbye to her husband. Kelso cleared his throat to let them know he was coming, then drew to a halt and raised the tips of his fingers to the brim of his hat.

'Good morning, ma'am.'

She offered him a brief, uncertain smile. She was dressed for travel in a tan-colored two-piece suit edged with black trim, and a white blouse buttoned to the throat. 'Captain,' she said.

'Nasty-looking wound,' the general commented with a glance at Kelso's ear.

'The post surgeon assures me I'll survive, sir.'

'Glad to know it.'

'With your permission, then . . . ?'

Crook nodded. 'Permission granted.' But for just a moment then it looked as if he would say more, until the moment passed and he merely nodded and muttered, 'God speed.'

While Crook helped his wife climb

up beside her driver, Kelso went back to his horse, mounted smoothly and then gave the order for his men to do likewise. They were such proficient horsemen that they mounted in unison and made the action look fluid, almost a thing of beauty. Then Kelso organized the men so that they would ride flank, swing and drag on the ambulance, with Kelso himself taking the lead and Lew Eden forging out ahead to scout the lay of the land.

At last Kelso's voice rang out across the parade.

'Company C . . . For — ward!'

As they approached the gate, Kelso saw the Apache scout, Peaches, ride in from the direction of town. As Peaches walked his mustang past, Kelso offered a nod of greeting. The Apache only looked back at him with something akin to pity — or as close to pity as an Apache was ever likely to come.

Outside the married quarters, General Crook was joined by Major Hackett. As the bustling strains of

153

Reveille floated across the fort, Hackett said, 'I hope I'm not speaking out of turn here, General, but there will, of course, be hell to pay if this goes wrong.'

'Even if it goes *right,*' Crook replied, 'it will be a long time before I can justify it to myself.'

He turned and went back into the quarters he had so recently shared with his wife, his shoulders slumped, his whole bearing that of a man who has suddenly aged beyond belief.

* * *

As the day grew older, reached its zenith and then headed for dusk, the border country alternated between broad, sweeping flats and pine- and oak-covered mountains, grassland and desert.

A little after noon Lew came riding back in from the ochre, steppe-like hills to the east to report that everything seemed quiet. But as he turned his horse around and fell in beside Kelso he said, 'You feel it too, don't you?'

'Feel what?' Kelso asked innocently.

Lew chuckled, a low, deep sound. 'They's somethin' wrong with this business, Cap. Somethin' that doesn't add up.'

Kelso nodded. 'Yup. I feel it. Nothing definite, just . . . well, like you said, an instinct. I just don't know what to make of it.'

He cut his gaze away to the right, where the distant, powder-blue bulk of the Sierra Madre Occidental shouldered toward a sky that was only slightly paler in hue.

'Maybe it's a test,' he hazarded. 'Crook wants to see how we make out, getting his wife to Lukeville.'

'It's a hell of a test,' countered Lew. 'Sendin' her out into the middle of Indian country.'

'You got a better suggestion?'

'Not right now. But I'm workin' on it.'

'Well, don't take too long. I want to

know what the hell we're being set up for.'

Around them the country was stippled with palmilla, jojoba, pitahaya and desert ironwood. On first inspection it seemed devoid of life. Life was out there, though, in the shape of rabbits and hares, deer and coyote, wild boar, wild rams and even the occasional bear.

At the end of the day two of the men went out to see what they could shoot for supper. A rope corral was rigged up and Lane Carr checked the horses over. A couple of the mounts were found to have loose shoes, and Porter Fitch, the one-time blacksmith who now carried a burlap sack filled with a hammer, shoes and nails, quickly made repairs.

That night they dined on a stew of deer meat. Mary Crook helped out as much as she could, and the men took an immediate liking to her because of it. She was strong, determined and capable, and wanted to make sure she handled her share of the chores.

After supper Kelso went across to the ambulance and found her stitching a sampler by a turned-low lantern.

'Good evening, ma'am. How are you bearing up?'

'Fine, thank you, Captain.' She stopped sewing and looked out at the growing darkness. 'It's a Godforsaken land, though, isn't it,' she remarked.

'I suppose that's one word for it,' he allowed. 'But it won't always be like this.'

'No?'

'No, ma'am. Once the Apaches have been subdued, the land will be opened up.'

'I can't think why. Who would possibly want to live here?'

'You'd be surprised. This may look like a wilderness, but there's good, fertile land to be had hereabouts. And of course, there's wealth to be had from beneath it, too.'

'Oh?'

He nodded. 'Gold, silver, copper, lead and maybe more besides. As soon as the Apache goes, the speculators will be all over it.'

'You don't seem to approve.'

He looked at her. 'No, ma'am, I don't. Not if it means the end of a way of life for one society so that another can get rich.'

She set her needlecraft aside. 'You interest me, Captain. Tell me something about yourself.'

'There's not all that much to tell,' he replied uncomfortably. 'And what there is would likely send you to sleep.'

She laughed, a pleasant sound in such otherwise cruel terrain. 'I'm sure that isn't so.'

'I was born in Columbus, Ohio,' he said.

'Then it's a very small world, Captain. George was born in Dayton.'

'My family originally came from Scotland,' he continued. 'The Isle of Arran, to be precise, and a place of rare, rugged beauty, so I've been told. I was educated at Dartmouth College — '

'Not West Point?'

'No, ma'am.'

'That has held you back,' she noted with surprising insight.

'I suppose it has, at that.'

'George was educated at the United States Military Academy . . . but he graduated practically bottom of his class.'

Kelso smiled at her. 'For the general's sake, I'll pretend I didn't hear that, Mrs. Crook.'

She laughed again. 'You know, you remind me of him,' she confided. And then, right out of the blue: 'My husband is a good man, you know.'

He frowned at her. 'I've never heard anyone say otherwise.'

'No. And you won't. But . . . sometimes he has to make hard decisions. Decisions which do not always make him popular. But that is the price you pay when you take on such a heavy responsibility.'

'Of course.'

'He is a good man,' she repeated, 'and he wants only to end all this senseless violence as swiftly as he can and establish a lasting peace.'

'Well,' Kelso said diplomatically, 'if anyone can do it, it's the general.' He stepped back a pace. 'Now, if you'll excuse me, ma'am, I'll go and check on the sentries.'

'Is there any need for sentries, Captain?' she asked. 'I was under the impression that the Apaches never fought at night. Something about the possibility of dying in the dark and not being able to find their way to the afterlife.'

'A lot of people have lost their hair subscribing to that old saw,' Kelso replied. 'But you'll be safe enough with us, ma'am.'

Out beyond the glow of their small campfire he checked on the sentries and was pleased to find that each man was on the alert and taking his duties seriously. He was on his way back into camp when Lew ghosted near-silently out of the darkness to intercept him.

'Take a look, Cap,' the half-breed said softly.

Kelso followed his pointing finger, saw nothing at first, only the empty darkness. Then —

'What *is* that?'

'A campfire,' said Lew. 'A long ways off, granted . . . but it means someone else is out there.'

'Apaches?'

'I wouldn't care to take the chance that it's *not*.'

'So what do we do? Hit them before they hit us?'

Lew shook his head. 'Too risky, an' these boys o' yourn got no night-fightin' experience to talk of. Best just keep our distance an' let them keep theirs — at least for now.'

'All right. But you'd better pass the word for the men to be extra vigilant tonight.'

'Yo.'

The night passed without incident, and the next day turned out to be a more or less identical copy of the one that preceded it, except that now the trail took them through lush valleys and timbered thickets where the harsh burn of the scrub-littered desert was just a memory.

As usual Lew scouted the land ahead, Kelso kept his men stationed around the ambulance, and though Mary Crook had a smile and a kind word for everyone, she now sat rigid beside her driver, displaying an unsettling kind of nervous tension.

Noon found them passing through a narrow, winding valley when Lew rode back in from up ahead. 'Seems clear,' he reported.

Kelso grimaced. 'It's that word *seems* that I don't much like.'

'Oh, it's all right,' Lew replied. 'I ain't spied no sign that makes me think we got any unpleasant surprises up ahead, but I think I'll take another pass at our back-trail. You know how sneaky the Apaches can be.'

He rode past the little column, back the way they'd already come.

The ambulance swayed and shuddered over the furrowed terrain. The men tried to keep their eyes everywhere, on the cabin-sized boulders that were spilled carelessly across the green-grass slopes and the odd stand of paloverde trees or pecans.

Kelso ran a palm across his glistening face. His ear was aching and to his dismay he was starting to feel that old, all-too-familiar need for a drink. To distract himself he tried to calculate the distance they'd already travelled — and that was when he heard the first distant pop of gunfire.

He swung his mount around, saw that his men had heard it as well and were already reaching for their Colts or Springfields. He galloped back along the line, aware of Mary Crook's worried expression as he went by, having no time just then to say anything that might set her mind at rest. But he did fix the ambulance's elderly driver with a white-gauntleted finger and snapped, 'Move!'

163

The driver, Corbett, didn't need telling twice. He slapped his reins against the rumps of his two-horse team and the ambulance pitched forward.

A moment later Lew Eden came galloping around a far bend, leaning low over his gelding's pumping neck.

And behind him came the Apaches.

Kelso abruptly drew rein.

Their excited yapping suddenly filled the valley. They were riding in a cluster, so it was difficult to calculate their numbers, but Kelso reckoned there must be at least thirty of them.

Thirty Apaches, loaded for bear.

Thirteen troopers, travelling light.

Kelso yelled, 'Shannon! Napier! Stay with the ambulance!' And then, ripping his saber from its scabbard and raising it high: 'The rest of you men, prepare to charge . . . and when we hit 'em, *hit 'em hard!*'

10

Lew Eden knew he should have paid attention to that itchy feeling he'd had between his shoulder-blades. It had never let him down before and it sure didn't let him down now.

He'd satisfied himself that there was no threat awaiting them up ahead. If there was going to be trouble, then, it would come from the rear, back where they'd seen the campfire the previous night.

So he rode warily back through the valley and out onto an amazingly fertile plain where the grass grew horse-belly high, his eyes everywhere at once.

The tracks they'd left behind them were plain to see, but no one else had passed this way — yet.

Lew reined in, took a pull from his canteen, rinsed the water around his teeth and spat off to one side. The uneasy feeling he'd had ever since leaving Whitethorn persisted. He scanned the land to the west, the scraggy slopes dotted with breeze-blown cat-claw, yucca and creosote bush. He felt that he was being watched, but the great open spaces nearly always did that to a man.

He had just more or less decided that he was imagining it when the deep boom of a long gun punched through the muggy noon air and a bullet slapped into the grass six feet to his left.

Startled, the gelding balked, Lew wrenched his .41 from leather even as he fought the animal down, and then there they were, coming up and over the far ridge; rusty, war-painted silhouettes against the brassy blue sky, yelling at the tops of their lungs.

Hascha's Apaches.

They came down the slope like water spilling down over rocky falls, and they were just about as unstoppable. But Lew didn't stick around to watch the spectacle. He made the pinto swap ends and got out of there in a rush.

He'd been lucky. Someone up there, maybe an excitable young buck out on his first raid, hadn't been able to resist taking a shot at such a fine target. But in so doing he'd deprived his brothers of the element of surprise — and given Lew a chance to cheat death that he wasn't about to pass up.

He gave the pinto its head. Behind him the Apaches came surging after him across the high-grass plain, yapping and yelling, a few sending hurried shots after him.

That was good — provided the sonsabitches didn't get lucky and actually hit him. The noise would give Kelso all the warning he needed that trouble was on its way.

Lew vanished back into the winding valley with the sound of pursuit loud in his ears. A few moments later he came around a wide bend with great clods of grass tearing up beneath the gelding's hooves, and there, some quarter-mile ahead of him, was the ambulance, rocking and pitching away from him at speed, and the men of Company C with Kelso at their lead with saber drawn . . . galloping hot towards him, ready to meet the enemy head-on!

There was something about the sight that, even in these circumstances, filled him with a raw, primal excitement; and as they came closer, closer, and then blurred right past him, each man with weapon drawn and mouth yanked wide in a scream of pure, cussed defiance, Lew wheeled his own mount back around to join them.

If the pursuing Apaches were surprised by the charge, they didn't show it, they just kept coming, until white man and red clashed in a confused jumble, and then all hell broke loose.

An Apache whose face had been transformed into some kind of death-mask by red, black and white war-paint threw himself at Reuben Brady and they went over the far side of Brady's rearing horse in a tangle. Brady lost his Colt in the landing, but his luck held. His opponent was barely more than sixteen years old, and because of that he had neither the weight nor the experience to hold the Texan down for long.

With a thrust of one lean flank Brady unseated him, threw himself atop the boy and tried to throttle him. The boy wriggled like a caught fish, raked Brady's long face with the nails of both hands and drew blood.

As Brady glared down at him he saw a kind of killing madness in the boy's eyes. There was nothing else in them, only the urge to maim and then slay.

The boy ripped a cheap trade knife from his belt and Brady saw it just before the brave could gut him. He threw himself away from the boy and the boy was just about to leap at him when Trooper Fitch rode past, swinging his own weapon of choice — his precious bag of hammer, nails and horseshoes.

He smashed the boy alongside the head and the boy performed something eerily close to a pirouette, a great spray of blood exploding from the back of his skull. He dropped into the black puddle of shadow at his feet, twitched once and then lay still.

While Brady went in search of his Colt, Kelso found himself fighting stirrup to stirrup with an Apache whose necklace of silver conchos flapped and flew wildly around him. The Apache screamed something unintelligible and then thrust forward with his lance.

The lance was nine feet long and ended in a wicked tip fashioned from mountain mahogany. Kelso used his saber to deflect the weapon, then brought his sword around in a hard, tight sweep that opened the Apache's throat and sent him back, loose and lifeless, off his pony.

Around him, the din was explosive: the bawling of men filled with a mixture of rage and fear that was impossible to contain; the shrill cries of scared horses mixing with the snap and crack of carbine and pistol; the fraught screams of men who were about to meet their maker and knew it. Kelso, teeth clenched as he thrust the saber away and ripped his Colt from leather, despised the sound, despised the need to kill even as he acknowledged that it was, as it was always likely to be out here on the frontier, bite or get bit.

Trooper Baranski's mount was shot out from under him. The big Russian threw himself from the saddle even as the horse collapsed with enough force to shake the ground around him. He landed awkwardly and tumbled to his knees.

Immediately one of the Apaches turned his charging horse toward him, leaning sideways in his blanket saddle so that he could brain the big Ukrainian with his ornate, flop-headed club.

Baranski saw him coming, leapt back to his feet, roared at the brave and grabbed the haft of the club as soon as it came within reach. He virtually plucked the Apache off his horse and swung him overhead and then down. The Apache crashed against the ground and as he did so something red and glistening popped from his ears.

Then Kelso was through the jumble of horsemen and out the other side. He swung his horse around even as another Apache drew level with him and struck him a glancing blow with the flat end of a tomahawk.

Although Kelso's hat absorbed most of the force, stars burst behind his eyes and he slid sideways out of the saddle. The Apache followed him down, leapt on top of him, his weight shoving the air out of Kelso's lungs.

The Indian brought the tomahawk up and back in preparation for the killing blow. Kelso stared up at him and wondered, stupidly, if his was the last face he would ever see.

Then there came a blast of gunfire that knocked the Apache sideways and off him. Kelso rolled hurriedly away from the body, reclaimed his fallen Colt just as more horsemen thundered around him, toward the main action.

Still dazed from the blow and the

pain it had reawakened in his sore ear, Kelso looked after them, frowning, thinking with disbelief, *They're ours. They're soldiers.*

Even as the newcomers joined the battle the surviving Apaches began to flee, instinctively splitting up and sending their ponies up across both slopes of the valley in all directions, still yipping and screaming for all they were worth.

Kelso, his fighting blood still up, drew a bead on one of them, a warrior with a broad, muscular back whose black hair, shot through with a distinctive steel-gray streak, flapped wildly around his head.

Hascha!

But then his aim faltered. He was a soldier, not a back-shooter; he couldn't bring himself to gun down a man in retreat.

Instead he switched aim, figuring to bring the Apache's horse down instead. He fired, missed, cursed the miss and then drew another bead.

But by then it was too late — the last

of the Apaches were disappearing over the tree-lined ridges to north and south, and the newcomers — men of the Sixth Cavalry, he now realized — were going in pursuit, even though Kelso knew from bitter personal experience that they wouldn't stand a snowball's chance of catching their quarry.

It was over, in almost less time than it took to tell. And as near as he could see, his men, gathered further down the body-littered valley, had survived it.

Reaction set in and a tremor ran through him. He suddenly felt tired beyond description. But there was no time for rest just yet; he heard other riders approaching slowly from some-place behind him, and turned to look up into the faces of the new arrivals.

General Crook and his scout, Peaches.

★   ★   ★

They stared at each other for a long moment, until the general said, almost afraid to hear the answer, 'My wife?'

Kelso shook his head to clear it and instantly regretted the action. 'I sent her on ahead with a two-man escort, to get her out of harm's way,' he replied.

'And then you and your men came back to lock horns with the Apaches,' said Crook. He was seated astride a tough little mule — always his preferred form of transport — and dressed in his cork helmet and long white duster. He presented such an odd, incongruous figure that Kelso wondered briefly if the blow to his head had caused him to hallucinate.

'Our orders were to hit them wherever we find them, General,' he said, swaying a little. 'Besides, we wanted to buy Mrs. Crook time enough to get well clear.'

'That,' said Crook soberly, 'was something I hadn't counted on.'

'What?'

Under the watchful eyes of Peaches, the general climbed down and led his mule closer. 'Are you all right, Captain?' he asked with what appeared to be genuine concern.

'Yes, sir. But if you'll excuse me, I want to check on my men.'

'Of course. I want to check on my *wife*.'

Still mystified, Kelso trudged back up the valley, past the bodies of red men and horses, to where Company C had gathered to lick its wounds.

'Lew?' he called.

Lew finished wiping something crimson off the blade of his hatchet and said, 'A little the worse for wear, Cap, but otherwise all present and correct.'

Lane Carr cocked his fair head. He was hatless, his hair mussed up, and he, like all of them, was sweating hard. 'What's going on, Captain? Where did the Sixth come from? Not that I'm complaining.'

Kelso glanced back at Lew. Lew nodded. From the outset they'd known something about this mission wasn't right. Now Crook's all-too-convenient appearance seemed to confirm it.

'Beats the hell out of me,' Kelso said at last. 'But I promise you men this much — I'm damn'-sure going to find out.'

★　★　★

Pursuit, as Kelso had expected, turned out to be fruitless. The men of the Sixth rode back in a short time later to report that the Apaches had scattered, and at Crook's orders set about pitching a temporary camp and cooking up coffee. By then Lew had gone out after the ambulance and fetched it back, and the general and his tearful wife had enjoyed an emotional reunion.

While that was going on, Trooper Carr took care of the wounds Company C had incurred. These were mercifully superficial, and amounted to little more than a few nasty cuts, some bumps and a few tender bruises. Kelso cleaned himself up and then went back to the Sibley tent that had been pitched for

177

Crook and Mary.

He found the general and his wife sitting opposite each other on collapsible canvas camp chairs. When he cleared his throat to announce his arrival, Crook and Mary stopped holding hands and Crook rose to greet him. 'Come in, Kelso,' he said. 'We need to talk, you and I.'

'That we do,' Kelso replied grimly. 'Are you all right, Mrs. Crook?'

Mary stood, clasped one of his hands and squeezed it. 'I am fine, Captain — thanks to you and your men.' She smiled at him, but he made no move to return the gesture, and uncomfortably she turned her attention back to her husband. 'I'll, uh . . . leave you to it,' she said.

As she left the tent, Crook said, 'I believe I owe you an apology, Captain.'

'For using my men as bait?'

Crook's left eyebrow rose a fraction. 'You've worked it out, then,' he said.

'Not really,' replied Kelso. 'But that much, at least, was obvious. You sent us out — you sent your *wife* out — as bait to lure the Apaches in. That's low, General, and frankly, I don't give a damn who knows it.'

'I'm well aware of just how low it was, Captain,' Crook replied, flopping back into his canvas chair. 'It makes no real difference that Mary volunteered for the task of her own free will, knowing what we stood to gain if my plan had worked. I didn't have to take her up on her offer and put her at risk, and yet I did. But sometimes you must use whatever you can to get what you want.'

Kelso remembered something Mary Crook had told him about her husband. *Sometimes he has to make hard decisions. Decisions which do not always make him popular. But that is the price you pay when you take on such a heavy responsibility.*

'And what is it you want, exactly?' he asked.

'Peace,' Crook replied simply. 'I have been sent here to make peace and that is precisely what I intend to do.'

'By any means?'

'My actions might seem low, as you say,' returned Crook, 'but my motives were honorable. You mentioned to me that you'd had some trouble with a renegade called Hascha. Hascha himself is of little concern to me, but he happens to be a close ally of Geronimo. My hope was to lure Hascha out into the open with a target he couldn't resist — the wife of *Nantan Lupan*. I had Peaches go out and spread the word that she would be travelling to Lukeville under light escort. My plan then was to spring my trap, take the man prisoner, do my best to convince him of my good intentions and, through him, arrange peace talks with Geronimo.'

'You took a damn' chance,' Kelso said bluntly.

'And yet I took every precaution to minimize the risks,' said Crook. 'We left Fort Whitethorn less than an hour after you did. You were under our observation virtually the whole time.'

'I know that, now. We saw one of your campfires last night.'

'Our intention was to confront any Apache force before they could reach you,' Crook continued, 'and take them prisoner as peaceably as we could. I did not expect they would get the chance to attack you before we could take a hand, and even if they did . . . well, I'll be honest with you, Kelso. I expected that you and your men would attempt to outrun them. I never dreamed you would turn and fight.'

'Then you underestimated Company C, sir.'

'Quite so. Fortunately, no lasting harm was done — I hope. I understand that all your men survived the engagement?'

Ignoring that, Kelso said, 'May I speak freely, sir?'

'Please do.'

Kelso's eyes suddenly lidded. 'If you weren't a general, *sir*, I'd punch you right into next week for putting my men at risk.'

'And I'd deserve it,' Crook replied evenly. 'But now I'm going to tell *you* something, Kelso.

'My first impression of you was anything *but* favorable. You came bursting into Major Hackett's office unannounced, stinking of whiskey and looking as if you'd forgotten what soap and a razor were for. Afterwards, when I read your record, I saw nothing to make me revise that impression. You came west with high hopes of promotion, and when that promotion failed to materialize, you turned to the bottle. Don't bother to deny it. It's common knowledge around Whitethorn.

'Well, I have news for you, Captain. Sometimes life doesn't go the way we hope it will. And do you know what? That's just too bad. Because the only certainties in this world are birth and death. Everything else we just have to take on the chin.

'So — I looked at you, and what I saw was of a man who wanted to use any means possible to make his mark. A man who felt he was destined for better things and couldn't understand why those things never seemed to come his way. You, sir, needed to have some of what I perceived as bluster taken out of you. So I gave you the chance to create what you have been pleased to call Company C in the full expectation that no man worth the name would willingly ride with you. That, I felt, would teach you a lesson.

'However, I was wrong. To my surprise, fifteen men *did* trust you enough to volunteer for what promised to be very hazardous duty indeed. So maybe you had something more to you that was not obvious at first glance.

'But then again, what kind of man would willingly ally himself to a drunk? The answer, at least to my mind, was a man who thought he might *literally* get an easy ride, whose job would be nothing more than to prop you up when you were in your cups. So yes, Captain — I saw Company C as nothing more than bait. And you know what happened? Shall I *tell* you what happened?'

'*Do,*' Kelso said darkly.

'You proved me wrong,' said the general. 'All of you. You stood and fought when you could just as easily have run. You put Mary's safety before all other concerns. Your men followed you in battle and once that battle was fought your first concern was for their wellbeing.' Crook drew himself up. 'And that, Captain Kelso . . . is why I now salute you. Why I salute *all* of you.'

And there and then, he did just that.

Kelso was stunned. Although he was still angry at Crook's treatment, he saw also that he and his men had shown what they were truly made of.

Feeling that everything had been said, he made to withdraw. 'With your permission, then, General, I'll return to my unit.'

'Yes, of course,' Crook replied. 'Tell them I have the highest admiration for the way in which they conducted themselves, and will be stopping by to thank them personally before we return to Whitethorn. Your men deserved better at my hands, and I failed them.'

Kelso kept his expression neutral. 'We all make mistakes, General. The only crime is in not learning from them.'

'Quite.' Crook said, 'You know, my hope was to wrap up this business the best and least violent way I knew how. All I wanted was a chance to speak with Hascha, to get him to listen to what I had to say.'

'Your motives were good, sir. It was just the way you went about it that I object to.'

'Would you have willingly set your-selves up as bait, had I asked you to?' countered the general.

'Probably not. But it would have been nice to have had the option.'

'All right, Captain. I feel bad enough about that as it is, without you rubbing it in. But there's more, isn't there?'

Crook had seen it in his face, in the sudden light that had come into his hazel-green eyes.

'Yes sir, there is. You'll remember the attack on the stage to Fortuna, where the two sons of the man Addison Crawford were taken by Hascha?'

'Of course.'

'I told Crawford I'd get his sons back from the Apaches. Unfortunately I wasn't able to do that. So we all make mistakes, sir. Mine was in making a promise I couldn't keep.'

'I understand.'

'I'm not sure you do, General. Unless you've been through it yourself, I'm not sure any man can. It still breaks my heart to think that I wasn't able to honor that promise, in much the same way that I still think about those boys every night before I go to sleep.'

'Well, there's not much I can do about that. I can't send you across the border to get those boys back.'

'Perhaps not, sir. But I think it might be to your advantage to do so.'

Crook scowled. 'In what way?'

More or less making it up as he went

along now, Kelso said, 'Let's just say that, if we get what *we* want, sir . . . we'll make sure you get what *you* want, as well.'

Crook sat back, intrigued. 'This sounds disturbingly like blackmail, Captain,' he said guardedly. 'But . . . all right. I'm listening.'

11

Three men rode hot into the vastness of Sonora, pursued by a cavalry troop under the command of First Lieutenant Miller. Although an impressive flurry of shots was fired at the escaping civilians, none found their target.

After a while, as if realizing that he was not going to catch up with his quarry — plus the fact that he had already gone just about as deep into Sonora as he cared to go — Miller called a halt. He and his men sat their heaving mounts for a time, watching as the men they'd been after grew smaller and smaller, until finally the desert swallowed them whole. Then they turned and headed back the way they'd come.

About a mile or so later, the three escapees drew rein and let their own horses blow.

It had been a fine, noisy show. Anyone who'd witnessed it would certainly walk away with the impression that these men were no friends of the army; that the blue-coats had been chasing them for some reason, and not just because they'd crossed the line into Sonora.

Nathan Kelso took a swallow from his canteen. The water was warm as coffee, and he grimaced. But he had no doubt that *someone* had been watching the apparent confrontation, and was likely still watching them, even now.

The man sitting his mustang to Kelso's left was General Crook's scout, Peaches. At Kelso's suggestion and Crook's orders, Peaches had let it be known among Hascha's sympathizers on the Lolotea Reservation and others that the crazy man at Whitethorn, whose sons had been taken by Hascha's Apaches, had hired some men to buy his boys back for him. Their currency — thirty brand-new Spencer carbines in .52

caliber, complete with ammunition, seventy-five rounds for each weapon.

Peaches had come along now not only to broker the deal on Kelso's behalf, but also for insurance. To an Apache, any white men in this neck of the woods were targets. But white men with another Apache in tow were more likely to be a source of curiosity.

'Well,' said Lew Eden, to Kelso's right, 'I'm sure glad those boys back there were lousy shots.'

'All part of the plan, Lew,' said Kelso. 'If that little charade doesn't establish our *bona fides*, nothing will.'

Lew snorted. '*Plan?* You mean that half-baked idea you made up for Crook as you went along?'

Kelso shrugged. 'He *went* for it.'

'He's *desperate*.'

'So was I.'

'Well, you got what you wanted,' Lew said, leaning back in the saddle. 'Now let's just hope you can deliver.'

They rode on. Although Lew knew the approximate location of Hascha's camp, it was not their intention to find it, but rather to allow the Apaches to find them. And if they thought there were weapons to be had from the encounter, the Apaches *would* find them — sooner rather than later.

They crossed scrubby flats bordered by distant, gray mountains. The heat was fierce. They stopped often to water the horses and check their surroundings. The desert was quiet, seemingly lifeless, but Kelso knew better. He knew also that they were still being watched.

Lew, he thought, had been right. It wasn't much of a plan. But it had come to him in that moment that Crook owed them something more than just an apology and a few generous remarks about their courage. He had risked them for what he considered the greater good — a chance to make peace. If he could make it with Hascha, then just maybe he could make it with Geronimo, as well. And if Geronimo accepted the peace, then it was possible that all the other hold-outs would follow suit.

But he had used Company C to do it. He'd been willing to sacrifice them, if need be. And because of that he *owed* them.

Kelso had been determined to collect on the debt.

They rode deeper into Sonora, closer to the mountains where Lew believed Hascha had his camp. Kelso's belly began to twist in apprehension. He had switched his uniform for jeans, high-heeled boots and a plain gray shirt, and allowed his dark beard to grow out a little. He wanted to look like the kind of chancer who'd take a desperate man's money and attempt to trade weapons for two boys.

If Hascha saw through his deception, it was all over before it even got started. There'd be fighting, wounding, killing, maybe even torture if it really went the wrong way. But like Crook, Kelso could only allow himself to think of the greater good, what they stood to achieve if they *did* pull this off.

They were swallowed up by the foothills. Eventually the trail gave way to a run of grassy meadows studded with enormous oaks, and he found himself wondering what would become of this wild, rugged, mostly unspoilt country if and when peace *was* established. It was as he'd told Mary Crook; there was a fortune to be mined from this land, and the white man wouldn't be slow to exploit it. Unless, of course, Crook could make provision for the Apaches in some way, and protect them . . .

The day waned. Still they saw no one, not even one of the regular *Rurale* patrols. At length Peaches said they should make camp and gestured to a shallow basin of land surrounded by twisted, spreading fig trees that looked ideal for the purpose. Kelso nodded agreement.

Night fell rapidly, and with it the temperature dropped like a spent horse. They sat around their small fire and ate a supper of chipped beef and beans for which they had no real appetite. There was no conversation to speak of, until, about an hour later, Peaches suddenly announced:

'They are here.'

And they were.

Kelso instinctively pushed up off his blanket, shocked to the core, because it was one thing to hear stories about the Apaches' ability to move like ghosts, another thing entirely to witness it first-hand.

There were six of them, and they literally came out of nowhere to surround them. Some held ironwood bows with arrows nocked and ready to fire. Two carried long guns, old weapons that would more accurately be described as antiques. The others carried an assortment of scratched, time-worn pistols.

Kelso sat up slowly, careful to keep his hands away from his shell-belt, and he looked from one man to the next, seeking the distinctive steel-gray streak that would identify Hascha.

Hascha was not among them.

But these men were here for a purpose, otherwise he, Lew and perhaps even Peaches would be dead by now.

'*Dagot'e?*' Peaches said in wary greeting.

The Apaches just stared at them.

'*Ne yaa' ta sai' pas,*' said Peaches.

One of them, their spokesman, curled his lip. He was short and bow-legged, wearing a beaded necklace over his blue shirt, a breechclout, knee-high moccasins, a war-medicine thong. '*Netdahe!*'

To Kelso's surprise, Peaches only smiled. 'We are *not* intruders,' he replied in his own tongue. He said some more, his words coming fast, sounding ugly and guttural, as the Apache tongue is wont to do. Kelso recognized only one of them — *peshegar* . . . the Apache word for *rifle*.

He was telling the Apaches that they were here to trade and that they had rifles with which to buy what they wanted. But he wasn't telling the Apaches anything they didn't already know. The rumor he had passed around had already spread like ivy.

The Apache told them his name was Zaltana. Then he made a grabbing gesture and rattled off something more. Peaches got up, went over to Kelso's gear, slid his 'sample' Spencer carbine from its sheath and held it up, one handed. He made a fist of his other hand and then flashed his fingers six times. '*Kah-tin-yay*,' he said. He was telling them they had thirty such weapons for trade.

Kelso, watching this Zaltana, saw greed stir in the man's midnight eyes. A moment later the man made another gesture, snapped a clear command.

Peaches said, 'He says he will take us to Hascha, but he does not trust us, and wants us to surrender our weapons.'

Kelso and Lew exchanged a glance. Kelso was reminded of that old saw about being careful what you wished for. 'All right,' he said after a moment.

Under the watchful eyes of the Apaches, they slowly, reluctantly unbuckled their pistols and handed them over.

Zaltana told them to saddle up and once again they did as they were told. When they were finally ready to pull out, the Apaches fetched their ponies in from where they'd tethered them, swung into their simple buckskin saddles and spread out around them.

The Indians led them through the night at a fast walk. The land rose beneath them and skeletal trees thrust black silhouettes against a cold, purple sky. Time lost much of its meaning. Kelso tried to estimate how long they travelled, how far they came, but it was impossible to do with any accuracy.

Brush grew thick between stunted trees, as did agave, sotol and small, spiny cactus. As they climbed higher he discerned the shapes of juniper, madrone and mountain oak. Sometimes the trees grew so close together that they could only pass between them in single file, and even then it was a tight squeeze.

Nevertheless, Kelso paid special attention to as much as he could, knowing they would have to negotiate every one of these obstacles on the way back . . . maybe in a hurry.

He wiped his mouth with the back of his hand, badly wanting a drink.

Dawn was lightening the eastern sky when he finally sensed excitement among their captors. He sat up a little straighter, feeling glassy-eyed, and there it was, below him — Hascha's encampment.

It was a maze of small, hide-covered *wikiups* nestled in a long canyon whose slopes were shaded by majestic, spreading oaks. Alerted by their arrival, a pack of half-starved dogs bounded up to meet them, wagging their stringy tails and yapping excitedly as they circled the horses' legs.

The reaction of the dogs in turn drew Hascha's people from their dwellings. Men, squaws, half-naked children

. . . as soon as they identified the newcomers, all treated them to an openly hostile appraisal.

Zaltana and the others led their prisoners between lodges, toward the center of the camp. The sun was climbing higher and shadows were steadily retreating. Lew chanced a seemingly casual glance up across one of the slopes, then the other, thinking some more about Kelso's plan, wondering if it could possibly work and knowing that if it *didn't* . . .

Apache children scooped up loose sand and threw it at the hated white man and his half-breed companion. Their horses shied a little but kept moving. Apache men growled murderous threats or insults as they passed by, and Kelso began to realize for the first time exactly what he'd let them all in for.

At last their captors led them toward the biggest of the *wikiups,* which was set at the approximate center of the camp. At its entrance, a stocky man watched them come. Kelso felt his blood chill, for this was Hascha, seen up close for the very first time.

Hascha was an older man, perhaps forty, his black-streaked-with-gray hair worn to his broad, muscular shoulders. He wore a thin white shirt and white cotton drawers, a conch-decorated belt and knee-high moccasins. He had deep-set, near-black eyes, a prominent, hooked nose, high cheekbones, a too-wide mouth that was turned down at one corner in an almost perpetual sneer.

Kelso, Lew and Peaches brought their mounts to a halt before him and sat their saddles while Hascha treated each of them to a long, insolent scrutiny. At last he fixed Peaches with a suspicious look and said something in a low, gravel-laced voice.

Peaches nodded and said to Kelso, 'He knows why we are here. He says he has the children we seek. But before you see them he wants you to show him what you have to trade.'

Kelso did the best he could to mime, *All right if I step down?*

It must have been adequate, because Hascha nodded, his bronzed, lightly pocked face devoid of all emotion.

Kelso dismounted, carefully slid the Spencer from its boot and handed it over. Hascha snatched it from him, hardly able to contain his eagerness, and inspected the cocking lever and trigger closely, keen to get the measure of the weapon. After a few moments he said something to Peaches and Peaches repeated what he'd said to Zaltana and the others, last night: '*Kah-tin-yay.*'

Hascha said something else. Peaches translated, 'He wants to know where the rest of the rifles are.'

Keeping his eyes on Hascha Kelso said, 'Tell him they're hidden away, safe. Same with the ammunition. He can have everything once we've got the boys.'

Peaches interpreted.

Hascha gestured to the gun, said something else.

'He wants to make sure this weapon works, but it has no bullets.'

Kelso nodded. 'Tell him to fetch the boys and I'll show him.'

Peaches did.

Hascha studied him for another long, uncomfortable moment. Kelso felt his flesh crawl, but forced himself to hold the other man's stare. At last Hascha barked a command and Zaltana nodded and hurried away.

'Zaltana will fetch them,' said Peaches.

'All right,' said Kelso.

He mimed that Hascha should hand the carbine back. Hascha hesitated, reluctant to surrender such a prize, but then did so. Kelso turned to his saddlebags, reached slowly inside, drew out the tubular, spring-loaded, seven-shot magazine that fitted into the repeater's butt-stock. He held the tube up for Hascha to see, raised his eyebrows, nodded.

Warily, Hascha nodded back.

Around them, the rest of the camp watched on, fascinated.

Kelso dropped the carbine's lever, slipped the magazine into the butt of the Spencer, then worked the lever to lower the breech-block and put a rimfire cartridge under the hammer.

Hascha watched closely, memorizing everything.

Kelso pulled back the hammer. It went *cli-click*. Then he aimed the weapon at the bole of a nearby oak tree and squeezed the trigger.

The blast kicked the stock back into his shoulder and sent startled birds soaring skyward. It also tore a sizeable chunk out of the bark.

Around them, the watching Apaches made sounds of approval and excitement. Hascha's eyes lit up and he nodded, extended his hands, flexed his fingers, eager to try the weapon for himself.

Kelso, looking at him through the burst of white powder-smoke that had accompanied the blast, worked the lever again, and as the spent casing spat up into the air he thought, *This is it* . . .

He reset the lever, thumbed back the hammer — *cli-click* — and aimed the rifle straight at Hascha's chest. As he did so, several braves instinctively started forward in an effort to protect their leader.

Expecting as much, Kelso quickly raised the carbine to his shoulder so that the barrel was aimed right at Hascha's face. That froze them in their tracks.

Addressing Peaches without looking at him, he said, 'Tell him he'd better do like I say or I'll blow him straight to hell.'

Impassively, Peaches did so.

'Tell him a dozen men have followed us to this spot,' he went on. 'Blue-coats. They have surrounded this place and they will shoot down every last man, woman and child in this camp if he tries anything.'

Even as Peaches began translating, Kelso continued, 'Tell him he has nothing to fear from us so long as he does like we say. We're taking those boys back home to their father, to where they belong. And we're taking Hascha with us because *Nantan Lupan* wants to speak with him. That's all. *Nantan Lupan* wants only peace, and once they have spoken Hascha will be free to return here, unharmed, to consider his words. But if he or his men try anything, anything at all to stop us, there'll be a massacre.'

Hascha listened with rising fury. He was not afraid for himself. He was not afraid for his men, and certainly not for their women, who were seen as little more than chattels. But his camp was filled with children, and children were a valuable commodity, the very future of his people. He could not risk them.

He looked at Kelso and Kelso was amazed that the look alone didn't strike him dead. He could see that Hascha was wondering if he was bluffing. The man's obsidian eyes shuttled to left, then right, up across the wooded slopes, seeking an answer.

And that was where he found it.

With the need for subterfuge behind them, the men of Company C, also dressed in civilian garb, stepped out of cover and allowed themselves — and their weapons — to be seen by all.

Again Hascha stared at Kelso. Somehow the men this *pinda-lik-oyi* had spoken of had followed them here, unseen and unsuspected. Somehow they had taken advantage of the distraction provided by the *pinda-lik-oyi's* arrival and demonstration of the carbine to creep in close and position themselves around the camp in such a way that his, Hascha's, people could not fail to be caught in a cross-fire.

Hascha said something low and slow. It needed no translation. Still addressing Peaches, Kelso said again, 'Tell him I don't like this any more than he does, but I want those boys back, and if there's one chance in hell that he and Crook can make peace, he's got to swallow his pride and take it.'

'Best not push him,' muttered Lew.

'Just tell him, Peaches. And don't try

to flower it up. Let him know we mean business.'

Reluctantly Peaches passed the message along. He was just finishing up when they heard footsteps behind them and Kelso dared to take his eyes off Hascha long enough to look around.

An instant later he almost forgot to breath.

Zaltana had returned, the Crawford boys with him . . . and their resemblance to their father was unmistakable.

They both had Crawford's bright, sad blue eyes and his dark-blond hair; his average build, too. They were dressed in deerskin shirts and breechclouts, and their smudged, tear-streaked faces were already burned dark by near-constant exposure to the elements. The youngest looked a little dazed by what was going on. The other one looked up at Kelso and tried not to cry.

'Are you takin' us home?' the boy, Ira, asked.

Kelso nodded. 'Your pa's expecting you.'

The nine year-old's eyes widened a fraction. 'Pa? Pa's dead.' And he did sob a little, then.

'He's alive and well and wants you two back,' Lew assured them. 'And we're gonna take you to him.'

Seized now by a sense of urgency that could no longer be denied, Kelso put his eyes back on Hascha. 'Peaches — tell him to tell his people that he's riding out with us, and they better not do anything to stop us because if they do, a whole bunch of 'em will die for no good reason . . . and Hascha will be the first to fall.'

'And then?' asked Peaches.

'Then,' said Kelso, 'we do our damnedest to get back to Whitethorn in one piece.'

12

It was an eternity before they were ready to leave. While fresh horses were fetched, and Kelso and Lew cautiously reclaimed their weapons from a furious but helpless Zaltana, the camp around them remained still and absolutely silent. Even the Apache children seemed to know that something was wrong, and stood transfixed, waiting to find out what it was.

At last Kelso, Lew and Peaches finished transferring their saddles to the fresh animals, each covering the others while they quickly fixed bits and tightened girths. Then Peaches swung astride and Kelso boosted young Joseph Crawford up into his lap, while Ira clambered up behind Lew and curled his arms tightly around the scout's waist.

That done, Hascha grudgingly mounted

his own pony and led the way out of camp with Kelso riding right behind him, his Colt aimed at the small of the Apache leader's back.

Every step of the way Kelso expected one or more of Hascha's braves to give in to temptation and make a try for him, or do something that would otherwise turn the tables or hinder their escape. He prayed it wouldn't happen, and almost beyond belief his prayers were answered . . . though he could see that the urge was strong within every Apache they passed to try something.

They were by no means out of the woods yet, but Kelso couldn't help but feel a fierce pride in his men. When he'd first put his plan to them they'd expressed their doubts, but at the finish not one of them had refused to go along and do his part.

Now he glanced from north to south, picking them all out as they kept their Springfields trained on the camp to make sure he and Lew and the others got out safely; Shannon and Carr,

Baranski and McGee, Brady, Quillan, Napier and the rest. These men would buy them the time they needed to make good their escape. Then they would withdraw and catch up, fighting every step of the way if they had to, but with orders to wound rather than kill when there was no other alternative. If Crook was to succeed in making peace here, he had enough ill-feeling to overcome as it was.

At length the camp fell behind them and Kelso stepped up the pace. They picked a path between all the close-packed trees, continued to descend through belts of juniper and madrone and mountain oak. The trees began to thin, they were hammered by the fierce heat of the new day but always they pushed on down toward the distant plain below.

None of them had slept in twenty-four hours, but for himself, Kelso was too keyed-up to feel even remotely tired. They'd taken a heck of a chance, but so far at least, it had paid off. And with every mile they put between them and Hascha's camp, they drew closer to the border, and the relative safety of their own country.

He was thinking that when Hascha suddenly yanked his reins to the right and broke away from the small column.

He aimed his horse for the cover of a boulder-field a couple-hundred yards to the south, and Kelso knew that if he made it into that maze, he'd be lost to them in a matter of minutes.

Kelso couldn't let that happen.

Shoving his Colt away he went after the Apache.

Hascha was halfway to the rocks when Kelso drew level with him. The Apache glanced sideways at him, his streaked hair bouncing around the twisted grimace of his face, and he did the last thing Kelso expected him to do — he sawed cruelly on his reins and stopped his mount dead in its tracks.

Kelso overshot him, drew rein, and while he was turning his mount around Hascha jabbed his heels into his own horse's flanks and the animal ran right at him.

The two horses collided with a heavy smack of flesh against flesh and Kelso's mount screamed and crashed over onto its side, taking Kelso down with it.

Hascha immediately leapt his mount over the fallen horse and tried to run Kelso down, but Kelso threw himself aside, and as Hascha wheeled his mount for another attempt he got his legs under him, ran to meet the Apache and made a reckless leap for him.

They both went over the far side of the Indian's horse and landed in an explosion of dust.

Hascha, fighting for his very freedom now, grabbed Kelso's shirt, yanked the man inside it up into his waiting fist. The blow exploded pain in Kelso's face. He fell backward, rolled sideways even as Hascha tried to stamp on him. Hascha landed hard, and Kelso used his own legs to sweep Hascha right off his.

The Apache landed with a bruising

smash, scooped up a rock, hurled it at Kelso. Kelso dodged it, charged head-down at his opponent, grabbed him around the waist and slammed him back against a dry, seamed boulder.

Hascha clasped his hands together, brought them down on Kelso's neck, once, again, again. Kelso took the blows, did his best to ignore them, came back up and hit Hascha right in the face.

Hascha weaved sideways, seeing stars. Kelso went after him, instead ran straight into a punch that sunk wrist-deep into his belly.

Hascha thrust him away, snatched up another rock, hurled it at him.

The rock sailed overhead, missing Kelso more by his own good fortune than anything else. He came up, bleeding from mouth, nose, a split of skin just above his right eye; and even as Hascha scooped up another rock and prepared to throw it, he hooked his Colt from leather, brought it up —

He thumbed back the hammer. It

snicked three times in quick succession, and then the weapon was ready to spit death and he, Kelso, was ready to make it do just that.

But —

But then he stared Hascha in the face: this man who had brought terror to the border country, who had killed all but one of the passengers on that noon stage to Fortuna; who had stolen Crawford's boys away from him and turned his life into a living nightmare. He looked at Hascha, the man who had led the attack on his small column so that he could take *Nantan Lupan's* wife as a hostage, who'd thought he was going to get his hands on thirty Spencer carbines to help him fight and kill his white enemies and who had relished such a bloody prospect. A man who had just now tried to kill him any way he could . . .

. . . and Kelso . . .

. . . Kelso let the Colt drop to his side.

Hascha, expecting death at any

second, couldn't entirely hide his surprise at the action.

Taking a chance, Kelso stuffed the Colt back into its pouch and held his hands out in a gesture that said, *It's over. No more fighting.*

Hascha held onto his rock, looked for just a moment as if he would take advantage of what he perceived as Kelso's weakness and throw it anyway.

'*Cap!*'

Lew's voice, coming urgently from the sloping trail, broke the moment and made both combatants turn his way. Lew jabbed a finger down toward the plains, and when Kelso and Hascha followed it they saw riders down there, a long string of them riding in column of twos — an enemy — a common enemy.

A *Rurale* patrol, riding south-to-north across the flats.

Lew and Peaches quickly heeled their horses into the cover of some timber. Kelso's horse and that of Hascha instinctively followed them. Kelso and

Hascha both dodged in behind a large boulder, from where they could watch the patrol go by.

The *Rurales* rode proud and haughty, resplendent in their gray *charro* uniforms and wide sombreros, their smart red ties and crossed bandoliers. If they should see Kelso and the others, it would go badly for them all. The *Rurales* policed the border with ruthless efficiency. They had no love for *Norteamericanos*, and even less for the Apaches they so despised. Out here they would be inclined to hang them all wherever they found them.

As they waited for the patrol to pass, Kelso felt Hascha watching him and returned his scrutiny, painfully aware that the Indian was still clutching the rock with which he had been planning to brain him.

But now Hascha was only frowning at him, as if trying to work him out. Maybe he was thinking about what Peaches had said on Kelso's behalf: *We're taking those boys back home to their father, to where they belong. And we're taking Hascha with us because Nantan Lupan wants to speak with him. That's all.* Nantan Lupan *wants only peace, and once they have spoken Hascha will be free to return here, unharmed, to consider his words.*

Was he wondering if he could really trust Kelso after all. Just now Kelso could have killed him, but didn't. Why was that? Why had the *pinda-lik-oyi* chosen to spare him?

It could only be because he had meant what he said.

Nantan Lupan *wants only peace, and once they have spoken Hascha will be free to return here, unharmed, to consider his words.*

Down below, the *Rurales* finally passed out of sight.

Kelso, still looking at Hascha, raised his eyebrows and allowed his expression to ask, *Well? Where do we go from here?*

By way of reply Hascha let the rock drop from his hand, dazed not so much

218

by the blows they had so recently traded as by his decision to take this white man at his word.

He nodded, still as wary as ever, then walked back toward the trees, and his waiting horse. Kelso watched him go and wondered if what he had just witnessed here was, at last, the beginning of the end.

* * *

George Crook stood at the window of Major Hackett's office, surveying Fort Whitethorn through tired, blue-gray eyes and stroking absently at his forked beard. As much as he hated even to think such a thing, it was beginning to look increasingly likely that Kelso's plan had failed, and worse, that by sanctioning it, Crook himself had sent seventeen good men to their deaths.

From his desk, Major Hackett studied the weary slope of Crook's shoulders, and guessing the direction of the general's thoughts said softly, 'It was Captain Kelso's choice, sir. His idea.'

'Of course. But I didn't have to go along with it.'

'Maybe not. But you did so for the best of reasons.'

A bitter smile stirred Crook's beard: Hackett saw it reflected in the window pane. ''Hell is full of good wishes and desires,'' the general muttered cynically.

'I'm sorry, sir?'

'Bernard of Clairvaux,' explained the general, turning to face him at last. 'It more or less translates as 'The road to hell is paved with good intentions.' And never were truer words spoken.'

'Ah.' Hackett pushed some paperwork about to look busy. 'If it's any consolation,' he remarked, 'I think the plan was doomed to failure from the outset. Hascha may be many things, but a fool isn't one of them. He was bound to see through the deception sooner rather than later.'

'Hascha is the least of my concerns,'

Crook replied testily. 'I can make another attempt to communicate with him and with Geronimo at any time. No, sir: I am having more difficulty with the decision I made to allow the men of Company C to risk their lives in such an enterprise . . . and the fact that it will now fall to me to tell your Mr. Crawford that we failed in our last attempt to rescue his sons.'

'We don't know that yet, sir. Not for a fact.'

'No. But it's been four days — '

Crook was interrupted by a knock at the door. Hackett called, 'Come.'

First Lieutenant Miller came inside, something akin to wonder on his face.

'Yes, Lieutenant?'

'They're coming in, sir.'

Hackett frowned. 'What?'

'Company C, sir. They're coming through town right this minute!'

Crook grabbed his cork helmet and made for the door. 'All of them?'

'As near as I can tell, sir.'

'Not a single man lost?'

'No, sir — '

But Crook was already gone, and Hackett was squeezing out from behind his desk to join him as quickly as possible on the parade ground.

As they went out into the new day enlisted men were crossing the parade from all directions, drawn from chores and duties by the news of Company C's imminent return. And even as Hackett finally caught up with General Crook, Kelso led his trail-dusted men through the gate and then angled his mount toward them, and Crook narrowed his eyes, counted the men, satisfied that they and Peaches had indeed all come back safely, and brought company with them —

Kelso walked his horse across to the waiting officers. Beside him rode Hascha, scowling at Crook and Hackett from beneath lowered brows but in all other respects perfectly passive. Peaches rode a short distance behind them, doubtless to make sure he stayed that way.

"General,' said Kelso, throwing up a salute as, behind him, Sergeant Shannon rode across the parade ground toward the guardhouse. "Major. As promised, sir, I am delivering Hascha into your care, not as a prisoner, but as a guest, for peace talks — whether he wants them or not.'

Crook opened and closed his mouth, shook his head. 'You did it,' he said in a curious tone. 'You actually *did* it.'

'Company *C* did it, sir,' Kelso corrected mildly. 'And we'd have been back before this, but we took our time in order to avoid all the *Rurale* patrols we ran across.'

With a nod, Crook turned his attention to Hascha and inclined his head respectfully. '*Skee-kizzen*,' he greeted, and indicating the admin block behind him, '*Ha 'ándáh?*'

Hascha, half-expecting some kind of treachery and not finding it, glanced at Kelso. Kelso nodded. Slowly, carefully, the Apache dismounted.

'Now,' said Kelso, 'if you will excuse me . . . ?'

Hackett waved a hand. 'Of course. Oh, and Captain?'

'Sir?'

'Well done.'

Kelso turned and rode back to his men, then dismounted, passed his reins to Baranski and waited while Lew Eden and Trooper Carr helped their young charges down from where they'd been sitting behind them. Kelso scooped the boys up, one in each arm, and began to walk smartly across the parade toward the guardhouse.

Before they were even halfway there, Shannon came back outside followed by Addison Crawford, who was squinting in the daylight.

No one had told the printer about the plan to rescue his boys for fear that it would build his hopes up only to dash them again. When he saw Kelso striding towards him with Joseph and Ira in his arms, he shook his head, unable to believe it.

IN THE HIGH BITTERROOTS

Will DuRey

They rode out as the snow began to fall. The seven men were to rescue a band of travellers trapped by an avalanche in the high Bitterroot Mountains. But once clear of the Montana township of Wicker, it's apparent that the on-coming winter blizzards are not the only threat to success. The swiftly assembled group members bring their own grievances and evil. Moreover, the mountain holds an unexpected threat for young Jess Clarke, and 'Doc' Hames.

A MAN CALLED BREED

Chuck Tyrell

They call him Breed . . . and when he is threatened with violence — because of his Indian heritage — he severely wounds Reed Fowley and seeks refuge in the desert. But Fowley, with his father and brothers, makes sure he's found — locating his homestead in Lone Pine Canyon, below the Mogollon Rim. They hire Robert Candless and a band of savage outlaws to kill him. Now, Breed and Blessing, his wife-to-be, along with his protégé Sparrow, must fight for their lives . . . or die.

And with the job done, his word kept, he turned and marched back to his waiting men, and as he went he looked at them, these soldiers who from now on were going to fight this war on the same terms as the enemy, he bawled briskly, 'Company C . . . *dismissed!*'

THE END

'Joseph?' he muttered huskily. 'Ira?' He took a step forward. '*Boys?*'

Shannon threw him a grin. 'Go get 'em, Crawford.'

'*Boys!*'

Crawford broke into a run across the parade, and his sons, seeing him come, this father of theirs they had believed to be dead, could control themselves no longer. Kelso set them down and they ran lickety-split to meet him.

'*Pa!*'

'*PA!*'

Kelso watched them go and swallowed hard. As they threw themselves into Crawford's waiting arms and they clutched each other more than hugged, he cleared his throat furtively behind one hand.

Crawford looked across at him, his eyes swamped, his lips twitching almost uncontrollably. 'Thank you,' he managed between sobs. 'Thank you, Captain.'

Kelso nodded. 'My pleasure, Mr. Crawford.'